Contents

Prologue   4

Book One
Son of Blue Streak   9

Book Two
Horse of the West Wind   46

Book Three
The Phantom Raider   79

Book Four
**Ghost Horse
  of the Oregon Trail**   126

Conclusion   167

PROLOGUE

I

THE sun was westering fast. A glint of gold lay on the mountains of the east, and the subtle movement of shadows began to etch the desert and Badlands adjacent to the Oregon Trail. It was exceedingly quiet. Away off, beyond Stone Corral Lake, the fabled Lone Butte country reared in grim isolation, the massive fluted outcrops, fantastic against the flaming sunset, seeming to guard what was once 'Wild Hoss Country'.

As the sunset hour approached, no more colourful place could be found in the whole of the Oregon–Nevada State Line, or in Idaho or Utah for that matter. It seemed that in Oregon, the mountains of the west deflected the shafts of sunlight so that they fell in vari-coloured streamers over the deserts and Badlands until the entire landscape quivered and glowed, and a mystic beauty lay over what was, in harsher light, a country of desolation.

Jim Blaine, now well past middle-age, and as familiar with the State of Oregon as he was with his ranchlands in the Santa Rosa Mountain area of Nevada, was thinking, as he rode along the trail, that never before could he remember having seen the distant Lone Butte country so clearly revealed. It seemed that he had but to reach out and touch the nearest butte despite the fact that it was still many miles to the north-west.

Screwing up his eyes the better to peer into the sunset, Jim Blaine decided the Big Butte was still more than a couple of hour's ride away.

A lean man, he managed to sit tall in the saddle in spite of his years, and rode his horse 'Blinker' with an ease that told

Ghost Horse

Stalli

JOS

First published in 1959 by
Hutchinson Publishing Group Limited
3 Fitzroy Square, London W1P 6JD

This paperback edition published in 1976 by
The Hamlyn Publishing Group Limited
London · New York · Sydney · Toronto
Astronaut House, Feltham, Middlesex, England

© Copyright Joseph E. Chipperfield 1959
ISBN 0 600 34007 4

Printed in England by Cox & Wyman, Reading

Cover illustration by Harry Bishop

TO ALL THOSE
Who

*In the State of Nevada
are endeavouring to bring
in legislation to protect
the last of the mustang
herds*

clearly of his life-long association with horses generally. He was a trifle grizzled, but tanned almost to the colour of an Indian.

Blaine was bent on a fishing expedition in Malheur Lake up north in the Harney Basin. Used to long journeys, he was travelling light. Apart from the horse 'Blinker', he had only the pack animal—a mustang that was as sure-footed as he was wise.

Altogether, the trek into the Harney Basin was something the wily mustang enjoyed since, like his master, he was no longer young.

The rancher was quite content to take things easy, determined to enjoy his vacation to the utmost. There was nothing back home to worry him. He had left the management of his well-stocked ranch in the capable hands of his son-in-law who would, one day, run it completely.

Blaine sighed with satisfaction, his blue eyes opening and closing as he rode, lolling back in the saddle, conscious of a pleasant state of security by the even rise and fall of the animal's rump. The sunset seemed to spill around him in a comforting glow.

He found himself recalling so many things, the names of so many places he had visited. More than these, however, he found himself thinking of the many famous wild horses that had made history in the Oregon–Nevada States—even those stallions that had come as far afield as Idaho and Utah.

There was Blue Streak, a grand stallion born in the arid mountains of Nevada. He was sure some hoss! Many old-timers, who generally knew what they were talking about had said that Blue Streak had sprung from the famous Apache 'Devil Horse' Diablo. He certainly possessed all the characteristics of an animal who would never submit to man, and which he could only have inherited from the Apache black stallion, Diablo.

Much that happened to Blue Streak eventually shaped the

destiny of that other great stallion 'Pahute'—or Ghost Horse
as he was to be known.

Blaine found himself recalling so many things connected
with the Ghost Stallion. To begin with, he was a horse of the
noblest ancestry. Son of Blue Streak, who himself had sprung
from Diablo, he yet had another claim to greatness. He was
reputed to have had as his dam none other than a filly bred
direct from the most famous of all wild stallions of the west—
Dark Fury!

All very interesting, thought Jim Blaine as he continued to
ride on into the western evening which, minute by minute, was
growing deeper in colour and tranquillity.

He was now approaching a small wash in the rough scrub and
desert. The whole area was desolate. It was truly a baffling
country, seeming endless in its monotony save where the lone
buttes broke the skyline like clenched knuckles uplifted to the
sunset sky.

The rancher began to straighten up in the saddle, his eyes
searching the ground ahead.

He nodded with satisfaction.

It was as he thought. He was approaching a waterhole.
Vague memories reminded him that once before he had
camped at this same waterhole. It was not until he pulled
'Blinker' to a halt and swung himself out of the saddle that he
realized just how tired he was.

II

The waterhole was typical of many another in that area of
scrub and desert. There were several washes running into it—
all, at this time of year, quite dry. The waterhole itself was,
fortunately, full, with an abundance of scrub and cotton grass
surrounding it. Its most distinguishing feature was an upthrust

of rock, about fifteen feet in diameter and rearing to a height of some twenty-five feet or so. At some remote period of its history, it might well have been a sizeable outcrop. Now, due to weather and age, it was but a forlorn reminder in sandstone of the ruthless passage of time—a finger of rock, shattered and weird in the evening light.

Jim Blaine decided that it was an ideal spot in which to set up camp. Being an old and experienced hand, he soon had his two horses hobbled on the rough grazing, and erected a small tent.

Within fifteen minutes, he had a fire blazing, and set about preparing his supper.

All this time, the westering sun sent long shafts of light streaming across the mountains. The indications were that the hour of sunset was to be one of quiet beauty and contentment.

As he prepared his meal, his mind constantly dwelt on the fabled Ghost Horse. He supposed the stallion must have been dead for almost a quarter of a century; and that reminded him unpleasantly that he was no longer a young man.

After supper, Jim dozed, grunting a little as he sought with the small of his back for a comfortable posture against the boulder.

The sun was now low down in the west, and the nearest of the buttes assumed the shape of some ancient castle, groined and pinnacled, with the warm glow of the sunset bringing every aspect of its shattered façade into sharp relief. Its fantastic appearance, rising so starkly out of the scrubland, gave a queer dignity to the western landscape, so austere and featureless. Soon the entire butte appeared to be smouldering with fire, with the first stars gleaming pallidly above it. A new moon lay over the serrated shapes of the Pueblo Mountains in the extreme south-east, while grey shadows seemed to spill out from the distant canyons.

One or two tiny dust-clouds appeared low down in the west. They seemed to hover over the distant butte for a few minutes, then vanished.

The stars became brighter. A little wind moved like a restless spirit across the scrub; afar off, some coyotes, bent on hunting, mourned aloud in what was clearly for them a lonely, a very lonely world.

Then when the day should have been fast fading in the desert, the evening light seemed suspended. Although the sun had gone, the afterglow streamed in long rivers of light over the skyline, and the nearest butte possessed the appearance of being little more than a mile away.

Blaine came out of his dozing, a sound having penetrated his consciousness. He was in that uncertain state of mind as a man who, having been afar off, suddenly finds himself back at his original starting point. He could not determine what had disturbed his previous tranquillity of mind.

He was still in a perplexed state of thought when he became aware of his two horses standing quite close to the camp-fire and showing every sign of alarm.

Then from a long way off it came again—a bugle-like sound!

The rancher was aware of fear. Yet he could not determine why he should be afraid. Such calls were surely common in this hinterland of scrub and desert, indeed, he had heard them often enough before in the past!

His whole body stiffened. That was just it! Such sounds were all of the past . . . the past of some twenty-five years ago. . . .

Maybe a little dust was whirling up from the foot of the butte; perhaps, after all, in this queer light and afterglow, it was all an illusion.

He continued to wait with rapidly beating heart. Once, a long time ago, he had heard a similar call, and it was followed by the stallion, Pahute, setting out on the rampage.

Now there was a strange, pent-up excitement in his waiting. He was wondering. . . . Over a quarter of a century ago the Pahute stallion had roamed the Lone Butte country. . . . A long time in the life of a man . . . an eternity in the life of a stallion.

The Pahute stallion was surely dead long since.

Book One
Son of Blue Streak

CHAPTER ONE

THE Pahute colt as 'The Ghost' was first known to the wranglers of Nevada and Oregon, was born on a wind-swept mesa west of the Pine Forest Mountains in Nevada. In the south-east was the dreaded Black Rock Desert, in the west, Massacre Lake. North, lay the Badlands of Oregon.

This was all wild horse country, the animals themselves being every bit as wild as the territory they roamed. Apart from the mountain areas, most of the terrain was arid desert, with here and there a lake set amidst a series of Red-River washes. Only the toughest of creatures could survive in such desolation, and the wild horse herds coming from this part of Nevada were typical of the country that gave them birth.

It was late spring when the Pahute colt first saw the light of day, and stood on very shaky legs beside his dam—a well-proportioned filly that Blue Streak, his sire, had added to the herd but a few months earlier. He was not much to look at in those first few days of his existence. True he soon learnt to jump and kick up his heels when the mood took hold of him. For the most part, however, he kept close to his dam who, since he was her first foal, took exceptional interest in him and in all he did.

All in all, life for the Pahute colt, on that wide, wind-swept mesa, adjacent to the Pine Forest Mountains, was one of ordered discipline, eating, sleeping and playing, with his dam constantly on the watch to see that he came to no harm.

It was the time of year when the birds, habitual to the locality, were teaching that season's brood to fend for themselves. Most conspicuous of these were two bald eagles who had their eyrie on a peak in the Black Pine range. Three or four times a day they came sailing slowly over the mesa, with two young eaglets in close pursuit. As the days passed, the young birds could be seen showing an ease in flight that resembled that of the old birds, their parents.

The eagles were responsible for one of the first hard lessons in the life of the Pahute colt. It was an event that remained closely secreted in his animal consciousness, coming to life on those rare occasions when something similar happened.

At the time of the first real experience, the foal was grazing on that part of the mesa where the western slopes broke away in a series of sandstone terraces. The foot of the mesa was little more than desert and scrubland, and a small herd of antelope came up to the terrace walls to shelter from the sun after visiting a nearby waterhole.

One of the more venturesome of the antelope had climbed on to a terrace where a patch of rough grass afforded a tempting morsel for his appetite. So engrossed was he in grazing that he failed to notice four winged shadows sweeping over the desert and finally brushing the terraces.

It was one of the young birds who first disclosed interest in the grazing antelope. He broke away from the spiral of air on which the others were gliding, and without warning, went into a stoop, sweeping low over the terrace with his tail feathers depressed to enable him to go into a side-spin should danger threaten him.

His sudden glide attracted the attention of the young horse who ceased grazing. With head held high, he watched, trembling a little as he beheld the other birds wheeling slowly above the plateau, obviously intent on seeing what was attracting the eaglet's attention.

What happened next badly startled the foal. The two old birds, with the remaining eaglet in close attendance, came suddenly gliding down on a strong current of air. They passed low over the foal's head before sailing along the terrace. There was, at that moment, a startling interplay of sunlight and shadow as a wisp of cloud drifted past the sun. Other drifts of vapour followed, and so intermittent were they that it was difficult at first to determine which were cloud shadows and which were those of the eagles.

The antelope, however, was in no doubt.

After his first glide over the terrace, the young bird investigating the ledge, gave a gruff bark like that of a dog and turned back into the air streams. It was that call of his that excited the other birds, and in a matter of seconds, a concerted attack was made on the defenceless antelope.

The old birds were most adroit at this type of thing. Their glide along the terrace wall was that of restrained power, coupled with deadly intent to drive the antelope from the security of the overhang under which it was sheltering.

Fortunately for him, the eagles experienced difficulty in reaching him. Whilst the upper part of the wall shelved outwards, the floor below sloped at an inward angle with the result that the creature was fully protected from any attempted assault from above. Moreover, the shelving wall shut off the flow of the air currents, and made it necessary for the eagles to beat their way clumsily to and fro.

They thus lost the impetus that had characterized their glide along the edge of the terrace. They could only penetrate the acclivity for a short distance and then swing about to make another attempt.

It soon became clear that so long as the antelope kept close to the inner wall, the old birds could not reach him.

Meanwhile, the Pahute foal, held motionless by a curious fascination at the eagles' constantly repeated efforts, began to experience fear. He wanted to run off and seek the security of his dam's flank.

Now, the cloud shapes racing across the vista of desert and scrubland served to bring into sharp relief the outflung arm of the Pine Forest Mountain range, and the far-off glint of Massacre Lake. Droves of wild horses seemed dotted over the scrub, while at the very edge of the mesa itself, no longer in shadow but clearly defined in a pool of sunlight, a herd of antelope made a pattern of speckled movement, against the yellow background.

Sunlight and shadow continued to race across the mesa, the mountain range and the desert. As the old eagles, with the two young birds gliding behind them, thrust upwards to make yet another turn along the terrace, the herd of antelope broke into startled movement.

Instantly, the eagles' attention became focused on this new point of interest, and this was the salvation of the deer sheltering on the ledge under the overhang.

The Pahute colt, however, was now so frightened that he whinnied. Swinging in wide arcs above his head, the eagles went driving past, and having separated one timid yearling from the herd of deer, slew him within a few minutes of the attack. Even as the remainder of the herd stampeded off in the direction of the distant wild horse bands, the creature on the terrace trotted off by a circuitous route and was soon racing after his companions.

In the meantime, the young horse had attracted the attention of his dam who stood close beside him while the eagles feasted on the carcass of the slain antelope. This was no unfamiliar scene in her eyes. She had witnessed it happening over and over again. It was an old, old lesson as far as she was concerned, the lesson of the strong triumphing over the weak. Moreover, it was a lesson her foal should learn, and remember, only in his case, he must be the one to triumph.

The filly finally tossed her head and led her foal away from the scene. He followed meekly enough—the terror gone from him the instant his mother stood at his side.

She need not have feared for the lesson she hoped he had learnt. The significance of what he had witnessed had been ruthlessly impressed upon him. Never again would he behold an eagle cleaving the skies and not remember. Never would he forget that to live, he, like others born to the heritage of the wild, would have to live by the law of the wild. Only the strongest survived!

And the days passed in sunshine and shadow on that high tableland adjacent to the Pine Forest Mountains and the dreaded Black Rock Desert.

CHAPTER TWO

HORSE wranglers had been operating north-west of the desert Badlands, and as a result, isolated bands of wild horses had penetrated far into the area of the Pine Forest Mountains. The bleached grassland and grey sage was not the best of grazing, but the wranglers had not travelled so far north-west, and the herds were less inclined to stampede at the first sign of movement in their direction.

Unfortunately for the horses, other less desirable creatures had moved north-west also, and with them, the greatest menace of all—the mountain lion.

One such creature—an ancient animal—battle-scarred after many encounters with wild stallions, bears and the like, began a complete and, for him an ominous sign, a very thorough investigation of the very mesa upon which Blue Streak's herd roamed and grazed at leisure.

The mesa itself was quite a considerable stretch of upland, deeply canyoned on the east and north, and rising to a height of some four thousand feet. The southern and western slopes slanted and heaved into terraces all honeycombed with caves in which many wild creatures sought refuge and reared their young.

Viewed from the waste of Black Rock Desert, the mesa was little more than a vari-coloured tableland, thrusting in a north-westerly direction towards the Pine Forest Mountains. At one point, lying in a deeply recessed canyon between Pahute Peak and the Division Mountain range, a river roared sullenly, an orange torrent that broke and surged against the red and yellow cliffs that contoured its course.

From time immemorial, the mesa had been the refuge and grazing grounds of the innumerable bands of wild horses that came up from the great Colorado plateaus in the south, and from the Pahute Mesa itself that probed down into the desert towards the sulphur springs.

As a result, it was also widely known to all those creatures who preyed upon young horses, and in particular to the mountain lions who seemed to know instinctively the route to take to reach the mesa, no matter how far they were from it.

Thus, the visit to the mesa—Blue Streak's province—was nothing unusual for the old lion of many year's battles. He had frequented it often enough before, but never since the stallion, Blue Streak, had brought his herd there for a brief sojourn before journeying on.

The lion took up temporary residence on one of the terraces, and found an investigation of the various caves much to his satisfaction.

Occasionally he made a kill, mainly of antelope, and it was fully two weeks before he turned his attention to the band of horses grazing on the plateau above.

Having acquired wisdom with age, the lion took good care to keep out of the way of Blue Streak and the younger stallions. He knew full well that to engage in a struggle with a fully-grown horse such as the leader of the herd might well end in defeat for him. The suppleness had long since gone from his body, and the frost of age had stiffened his limbs.

Even so, he was still a formidable opponent when roused. He could still leap to some effect, and his claws were still as sharp as knives.

His main disadvantage on the open mesa was the lack of suitable covering. There were no trees and very little scrub. Even the few rocky outcrops that were apparent were so shattered that it was difficult for him to find even a crevasse in which he could crouch unseen.

For the most part, therefore, he kept to the terraces, making surreptitious visits to the summit under the cover of darkness.

It was not long before he learnt the pattern of movement as

followed day by day by the young mares and their foals. Their
method of grazing was to move with the sun so that their heads
were protected from the heat. Moreover, they frequented the
few waterholes on the mesa at regular intervals—the last main
visit being just after sundown.

At the evening visit, they were always accompanied by Blue
Streak himself, and the lion knew that to essay a kill at that
particular hour would entail an attempt at segregating one of
the foals from the herd under the watchful eye of the stallion.

The old lion therefore bided his time, watching for more
favourable visits to one or other of the waterholes. He finally
discovered that the best hour of all was just before sun-up when
Blue Streak made a habit of making a general survey of the
mesa, leaving the herd much alone for as long as a couple of
hours at a stretch.

The lion's moment of striking came when the Pahute foal
was a little over two month's old.

It had been an exceedingly cold night on the mesa, with the
stars shining hard and brittle in a sky that was quite clear of
cloud. There was a little wind coming in from off the mountains
of the north, and shortly before daybreak, it had a bite in it that
caused the mares and their foals to close in together for warmth.

All through the short hours of darkness, the lion moved up
and down the sandstone terraces, a dark shadow amongst so
many other shadows. He constantly flaired the wind currents,
waiting for the moment when he could no longer scent the
stallion. Despite the instinct of caution, constantly probing
him into almost complete immobility, he was swayed by an
even stronger impulse to go up on to the open mesa and make
for the waterhole most favoured by the mares.

Unfortunately for him, Blue Streak was very much in
evidence. An hour or so after midnight, the stallion had picked
up the lion's scent. Throughout the long years of the existence
of the wild horse herds in the North American continent, the
mountain lion, and the grizzly bear, had been their most

defiant and formidable enemy. Thus in the bloodstream of all wild horses was stored the reflexes of their ancestors—those horses of Arabian blood brought to the New World by Cortez, the Spaniard, who conquered the Aztecs and Peruvians. They knew by instinct when a lion or bear was in the immediate vicinity, and in the case of Blue Streak, he had been fully aware of the fact for many days, but never so acutely as now—on this night of the bright stars and the chill north wind.

With this knowledge constantly stirring in him, he kept very much on the alert, and soon the night was worn by his pacing into the first glimmer of a new day.

The moon had set long before the night began to lift slowly from the plains and hills. Gradually, the sage flats and broken land north-westward to Massacre Lake, started to take on a definite shape and colour, at first appearing only faintly grey, but none the less clearly visible from the mesa. The stars grew frail and died as a mocking bird called. Over the ridges and peaks of the Pine Forest Mountains a transfiguration in crimson and gold was taking place.

Soon now, the sun would be up!

This was the hour when the mares and their foals went to the waterholes. Already, some were moving up out of the hollows—quietly and without haste—the foals keeping close to their dams' flanks, except one—Pahute! He had glimpsed his sire standing away off on the precipitous edge of the mesa, and moved by curiosity, for the stallion was seldom nearby at this hour approaching sun-up, the foal trotted over to him with mincing steps that were softened by the dew on the coarse grassland.

Blue Streak gave no indication that he was aware of his presence. Something far more important than the foal had gripped his attention.

The lion, acutely conscious that the hour when the mares and their foals would be at the waterholes, made a silent escape from the cave where he had remained for so long hidden. The morning breezes were veering from north to north-east, and since they were sweeping straight off the mesa and not reaching him as he moved along the terraced walls, he could not tell whether or not Blue Streak was still on guard.

The stallion saw him the very instant the lion broke cover and moved along an unprotected scree slope in an effort to reach another ledge that went up at a steep angle to the summit of the main escarpment.

Blue Streak did not move, nor did he betray any indication that he was aware of the lion's definite manœuvre to gain the summit.

The young foal, watching him so intently, seemed caught up in that same attitude of frozen immobility. His ears were thrust forward a trifle in his anxiety to interpret correctly his sire's mood, his curiously tinted tail half-raised and faintly moving in the air currents. There was some primitive instinct within him that warned him of danger. At the same time, he was conscious of a rare sense of security by reason of the very closeness of Blue Streak.

Meanwhile, the stallion retained his attitude of silent scrutiny. His eyes, gleaming angrily, never left the moving shape of the lion for a single instant. The ledge, upon which the beast now stood precariously, was heavy in gloom, being in the rainy seasons more of a gully than a track leading to the summit. Even so, the stallion had not the slightest difficulty in following every step the marauding animal took.

By now, most of the mares and their foals were out of the saucer-like hollows and congregating in the vicinity of the waterholes. The lion still had no idea that he was under direct surveillance by Blue Streak, and started to lope with a greater display of energy in the direction of the summit ridge of the mesa.

The sun was coming up over the massed mountain ranges of the east in waving streamers of gold. Moment by moment, the fiery conflagration of the heavens was growing in colour and intensity. A mocking bird called out loud and clear from a nearby clump of scrub; somewhere—over in the desert surrounding Summit Lake—a young antelope uttered a harsh cry of fear as two winged shapes flew high above it, sending their shadows sweeping over the floor of the desert as, in their soaring, the rim of the sun caused a sudden flow of light to spill from out of the east.

For a second, the antelope's cry vibrated in the ears of the lion. He paused, hesitating, in the very act of leaping on to the ridge above. It was a moment tense with uncertainty. He did not know whether to leave the mares and their foals unmolested and go off in search of easier game. One leg was half-raised as he turned his head to see out over the western Badlands, his ears set to catch any further cry the antelope might make and thus set more accurately the distance he was away.

The cry never came, and the lion without further hesitation, leaped on to the open mesa.

His leap was made at the very point where he knew one of the most favoured waterholes to be. Nor was he mistaken. The waterhole was less than a couple of hundred yards away, but between it and himself was the stallion, Blue Streak, and the very young Pahute foal.

Taken by surprise, his reactions were, none the less, instantaneous. He swung away from the waterhole, and defying the stallion's threatening move in his direction, made straight for the foal.

Blue Streak went thundering towards him, while the mares and their foals in the vicinity of the waterhole stood in stupified amazement.

The Pahute foal, menaced by the lion, realized his danger just in time. However, instead of turning and racing off, he reared and threshed his fore-feet—a habit that was to become characteristic of him in the years ahead.

His unexpected attitude confounded his would-be attacker,

causing him to falter to a stop, crouching low to the ground.

That proved the lion's downfall. Blue Streak was on him like a dark thunderbolt. At the same moment, the young foal brought his hooves crashing down within a couple of feet of his head, while to add to the confusion, the mares and their foals began a stampede from the waterhole.

The lion was not only startled by the unexpected turn of events, but for a second or two quite unable to make any decisive attempt to protect himself. When he did respond to a swift awareness of danger, Blue Streak was already a rearing, snorting outline above him.

Snarling with savage intent, the lion rolled on to his back, his entire body wrinkled as his muscles went into action. He succeeded in rolling away as Blue Streak's hooves pounded down, his fore-paws striking upwards, then down, missing the stallion's chest by a matter of inches. It was then that the old lion encountered yet another source of danger. The foal lunged at him.

For one short instant he saw the foal plunging towards him, and even then, with Blue Streak clearly bent on making another attack, he thrust out one paw to rip the young horse from flank to fetlock.

Too late, however, that thrust: too late also to remedy the false position in which he now found himself. The foal was on one side of him and Blue Streak on the other.

It was the stallion that finally brought him stumbling and writhing to his feet as the foal went careering away in terror at his sire's shrill cry of uncontrolled rage.

The lion beheld once again the silhouette of the horse rearing over him like an enormous shadow of threshing limbs starkly revealed against the red flaming of the dawn sky. He saw too, in that last moment of conscious sight, some clouds passing high over the mesa and the pinioned outline of an eagle.

Then the hooves crashed down upon him, driving deeply into his body which seemed to rebound with the impact.

The creature made two further upward slashes with his paws, followed by yet another attempt that was too weak to save him from death.

A second later, he lay inert beneath Blue Streak's pounding hooves, while the stallion's scream of triumph went echoing across the mesa and out into the streaming blood-red glow of the new day. . . .

CHAPTER THREE

SUMMER in the Nevada Badlands was the dry heat of a sun that rose early and set late, scorching everything until the grass and sage were bleached white, and the small lakes dried up. It was then that all living things sought shelter where the mountains cast purple shadows upon the immutable desert. Distance was but a haze of shimmering heat waves, with here and there a frowning mass of red rock, riven and split by the countless years that had gone into their making and ultimate destruction.

Always in summer, there was more harsh colour in Nevada than could be seen in any other State, with the few mountain rivers red and sullen as they flowed between high-flung canyon walls that were as barren as the very desert from which they reared.

Night also was a thing of heat, with the stars seeming so far off. Where the mountains were closely massed like giants on a fantastic backcloth, dark veils of shadow hung between the individual ranges, and always at night, was the intensified crying of a river, glistening silver now instead of running red as it flowed endlessly on to fall in a racing, shouting cascade into an abyss that added to its voice and stature.

Blue Streak had already spent five summers in the Nevada Badlands, and always, before the dry heat came, he moved off the mesa of his spring-time grazing, and went down into the desert to trek to another grazing in Red River Canyon— a southerly spur of the Pine Forest Mountains. It was reasonably good country for a herd of horses. The grass though sparse, was yet sufficient to support the stallion's many mares, and the deeply recessed canyon itself, with its red river, gave adequate protection from the sun, and good watering.

The stallion was a good leader. His small hoofs were hard'
and his muscles well developed so that he was able to lead
the way across rough rock country that would have defied the
efforts of many another animal.

Unfortunately for Blue Streak, he was not entirely unknown
in western Nevada. Many tales were told about him, and his
habits too were not unknown to some of the wranglers that
came from the east. Indeed, there had been an occasion, not
more than a couple of years back, when three ranchers of the
Indian Creek country surprised the stallion.

They made a bold attempt to round up the horse, and
while, after many hours, they succeeded in heading the stallion
and his herd into a blind canyon, piled high with rocks, Blue
Streak had leapt over obstacles with an ease that completely
confounded the men. More than that, he had trained his mares
to jump in much the same manner.

The result became 'wild hoss' history in that part of Nevada.
Just when the ranchers thought they had the herd and the
stallion himself trapped at the blind end of the canyon, Blue
Streak swung about without any warning whatever. Rearing
and plunging, and screaming with rage, he drove back on
the totally unprepared men. As they pressed their trembling
horses into a recess in the cliffs to escape being trampled down,
the mares and their foals came crashing and leaping over the
jumble of rocks and debris.

A yellow, acrid dust cloud rose, stifling them. The screams
and the racing herd, and the thunder of so many hooves, were
made doubly hideous by the echoes that were tossed up and
flung from cliff to cliff and back again. The stench of sweating
mares, and that of the ranchers own horses who were clearly
terror stricken by the unexpected turn of events, added to the
awesome effect of the scene.

The ranchers admitted later amongst themselves that they
had never been so relieved in their lives before as when they
beheld Blue Streak himself leaping after his mares to freedom.

Even if the men never caught a single mare, or foal, out of Blue Streak's band, they nevertheless had his measure. They knew that he was a fearless and wholly undisciplined animal, and that the only way to trap him would be to kill him. He was, as with all his kind, a stallion who preferred freedom to captivity, and to retain that freedom, would quite clearly die rather than submit to man.

One further thing too they knew—his description, which was quite exceptional. In one angle of sunlight, his colour seemed to be crane-tinted, clearly indicating his Spanish ancestry; in another angle, almost blue-black, with white stockings and blazed face.

After the return of the three ranchers to the Indian Creek country, and their story got noised abroad, many old-timers swore they would get Blue Streak, and not only him, but his mares as well. Certainly attempts were made to track down the stallion, mainly in the late fall or winter, but never could any experienced wrangler pick up sight or sound of Blue Streak. True there were numerous horse trails through narrow canyons and over mountain passes, but never a one led to Blue Streak's winter hide-out.

The stallion had chosen wisely and wintered way up north in mountains that rose from a gulched and tumbled mesa in a towering spire that was split in many places, each small pass possessing trails that led from north to south, and from east to west.

In a like manner, he had chosen equally as well his hide-out for the summer months. He realized only too acutely that his greatest enemy was man, and that everything he did must be based on that knowledge, and an adequate means of escape available should man suddenly put in an appearance.

It was exactly two weeks after his encounter with the mountain lion that Blue Streak decided to start rounding up the mares for the long trek to the summer grazing. The moment he responded to a subtle probing in his animal consciousness

was just after sun-up when he stood on the edge of the escarpment gazing northwards. Below the mesa, the vast sloping
terraces fell to the floor of the desert like massive steps, and
where the desert seemed to end, was a sloping valley of sagebrush, rolling grey to the mountains and the Red River
Canyon.

Even as he stood staring away across the many difficult
miles that separated the mesa from the mountain range, the
stallion flicked his ears as if he could already catch some faint
sound of the sullen voice of the river. At the same time, his
nostrils flared, and he could almost smell the lush grass watered
by spray where, most days of the year, a rainbow hung like
an arch over the canyon.

Blue Streak turned away abruptly and trumpeted to the
herd. Another instant, and the great round-up had begun.

The stallion's first move was to make a general survey of the
band. There was a suppressed excitement in his steady pacing
around the mesa, excitement too when he paused for a moment
to regard some of the mares. The herd was large, too large in
some ways. The younger animals might prove difficult on the
trek that lay ahead of them.

Then, seemingly all in a minute, Blue Streak was striding
from north to south, driving in those scattered animals that
were grazing on the south-eastern strip of the mesa. Soon his
striding became a steady trot that took him three times around
the mesa before he was satisfied that all the mares were together
and in a manageable position to drive down the winding tracks
to the desert below.

Shadows were now leaping over the upland that had nursed
so many of the foals as a few clouds passed high above. Down
amongst the scrubland was heard the faint yammer of a coyote
pack on the hunt. This sound was soon drowned by Blue
Streak himself giving a shrill scream that warned the band
of his final intentions.

A second later, with the stallion pacing swiftly along the

western flank of the herd, he headed the first of the mares towards the ledge-like trail that, in winter, was little more than a water gully.

* * * * *

It was well after high noon when the whole band was at last on the floor of the desert, some of the foremost animals already wandering off amongst the scrubland. Most of them could smell water from the river that flowed between the Division Mountain range and Pahute Peak, but before any of them could set off in search of the water, Blue Streak was amongst them. He was now intent on getting them on the move northwards, and was in no mood to tolerate disobedience. He ran backwards and forwards, all the time trumpeting his displeasure should any mare attempt a breakaway southwards.

The entire herd was very quickly pacing along a trail that, for a hundred years or more, had been the trail used by countless wild horse herds making for the main mountain watershed. The stallion, this time, was running alongside, keeping the band set in the direction that would finally bring it to the Red River Canyon.

Ahead, the ramparts of the Pine Forest Mountains rose like a fantastic barrier, wooded in parts, but on the higher slopes, disclosing the yellow and red colouring characteristic of the ranges astride the Nevada—Oregon State-line.

It was Blue Streak's intention to reach a small patch of fresh grazing before sundown, and as the afternoon drew on to early evening and the sun began to go down over the heights above Massacre Lake, the stallion forced the pace a little.

Then as the evening shadows blotted out the afterglow of the sunset, Blue Streak drove the band into a narrow canyon that possessed some rough grazing, and was watered by a small stream.

Early next day, however, the herd was again on the trail,

this time moving up through a narrow break in the hills. This was all mountain country, and somewhere within those deeply receding canyons, lay many of the inland rivers that might well be lakes, for none had any outlet to the larger rivers that flowed east to the Pine Forest Mountains.

The first of these many waterways was encountered that same afternoon, and towards evening, when the sinking sun brought an ever-changing display of colour to the uprising cliffs, Blue Streak, now at the head of the herd, brought the first of the mares to the very ramparts of Red River Canyon.

The long trek to the stallion's summer grazing, was nigh at an end!

*　　　*　　　*　　　*　　　*

With the swift gathering of night in the canyon, the band soon bedded down, some of the more venturesome colts moving off towards the red cliffs where they stood in groups, gazing about them.

It was quite dark when Blue Streak faced down the canyon, conscious that he had been joined by one of the colts. The stallion did not as much as give the smaller animal a glance. Thus, the Pahute colt—for it was he—sensed that his sire was not displeased, and like the older horse, the colt stood staring into the gloom.

It was still some time before actual sunrise that Blue Streak roused the herd and got the mares and foals once more on the trail. The stallion's movements possessed an urgency even greater than that he had shown the previous night. He was now determined to reach his summer hide-out within the next few hours.

Even as the canyon resounded to the steady pounding of hooves, all firmly placed, so did the east burn with the sombre fire of the dawn, but before the sun had risen, the herd, and Blue Streak, had vanished, trekking up into the greater canyon that thrust north-westwards into the vast upheaval of the Pine Forest Mountains.

The nature of the terrain was constantly changing. Rough scree and boulders gave place to red sand, broken here and there with scrub. Then the canyon widened, opening out into a tremendous basin, at the northern end of which flowed the Red River itself. All about the river, and far into the receding canyons that struck off both east and west, was the green of grassland and the purple of sagebrush, with a few stunted trees of juniper clinging to the almost perpendicular cliffs that rose a full four thousand feet above the main valley.

Beyond the river lay the glen of time-sculptured monuments, each one rising to a thousand feet or more, gleaming yellow and red in the mid-day sunlight, all boldly discerned, and none seeming less beautiful than its nearest companion.

Thus was Blue Streak's usual summer grazing ground . . . a canyon concealed in the heart of the Pine Forest range, and one which few men had visited in the countless centuries that had witnessed the monuments being carved and polished by the wind and the rain. . . .

A rainbow, quivering multi-coloured in the sunlight, told of the falls where the Red River fell tossing and foaming to a lower valley that thrust eastwards into the range towards the Quinn River and the dreaded Black Rock Desert.

Blue Streak, surveying the pleasing prospect of Red River Canyon was aware of only one thing. He was arrogantly satisfied at having reached once again, without mishap, this secret hide-out that was known to him alone.

CHAPTER FOUR

THE Pahute colt liked the canyon. It was more intriguing than the mesa, and the river was a continual source of interest. All the younger animals spent most of their time on its banks, for not only was the grass good to the tongue, but it was moist, and not at all dry and brittle as most of the grazing elsewhere. There were also odd moments when a stealthy movement gave to the grass a suggestion of life. Indeed, it *was* life that stirred in it. Rabbits, large and small, suddenly appeared and as suddenly vanished, with little more than a whisk of their skuts to dazzle the eyes of the startled colt.

And there was a new vitality that seemed to spring up, not only in the Pahute colt, but in all the other young animals.

As the days passed by, the Pahute colt and one or two others of about the same age, became exceedingly ambitious. They started to investigate the small side canyons, penetrating far into boulder-strewn glens, and attempting to climb ledges that only the antelope visited.

For the Pahute colt, this was joy beyond anything else he had yet experienced. His long, spindly legs, his tossing mane and streaming tail, would all seem part of the nervous energy he expended in his running. His legs always stretched out to their utmost limit, his whole body seeming to be on springs as time and time again he outpaced all of his companions, and quite suddenly turned back from the northern wall of the canyon that had been their objective, only to snake his way through their serried ranks while they were yet unable to break the turn of speed they were making.

Despite these moments of high-hearted endeavour, it was not all play for the Pahute colt. Quite often, he ignored those of his own age, and kept within close distance of Blue Streak.

GHOST HORSE

There was something about the great stallion that attracted him. He found it impossible to move far from the horse when the animal had taken up one of his familiar stances—that of standing like a sentinel on a high ridge of ground, and remaining completely motionless for an hour or more at a time.

Already the play of the winds about him, the deep, ever-shouting voice of the river, and the sight of cloud smoke over the mountains, made a little less difficult the sifting of the mood patterns. They were, after all, part of the mysterious pulse of life within him . . . the pulse that came from Blue Streak, and even farther back . . . from Diablo, the Apache 'black devil horse'.

Often then, when he was strongly aware of this throbbing pulse of life in his veins, he turned away from contemplation of his sire, and quivering with a strange desire, searched the high mountains at the head of the canyon, his nostrils widely flared as he sought to read the messages the wind brought from off the peaks.

His immature body would seem to fill out until he felt every bit the size of Blue Streak, and he would lower his head and paw at the earth. Sometimes he indulged in a short, sharp gallop, going round and round, finally snaking low as if bent on attacking a hidden adversary.

Then, as suddenly as it had begun, the quivering and the strange desire would be gone, and he became once more a very small and inexperienced colt, unable even to interpret the messages in the wind.

It was all so perplexing; but life, when such moods had departed, was all the more exciting. He would utter a loud neigh and leap off in search of companions, moving in a long, swinging stride, his head high and his nostrils flaring the breeze.

So, for the Pahute colt, began the long days of summer in Red River Canyon. The sunlight seemed never before so bright as now. It gave clarity to the high hills and escarpments; and always, as far as the eye could see, there was the splendid array of colours, some grey, some red, and some yellow.

Brighter than any of these, however, was the vermillion hue of the river as it rolled between the high cliffs towards the falls and the rainbow, and the valley of time-sculptured monuments that lay in the path of the sunset. . . .

*　　*　　*　　*　　*

After four months' sojourn in Red River Canyon, the Pahute colt began to show very definite signs of the horse he would one day become. He possessed a good depth of chest and a very firm back. His legs too were less spindly, and like Blue Streak, he had white stockings. His coat was now much the same colour as that of his sire having the appearance in certain shades of light of being steel-blue. His eyes were clear, and flint-coloured, and saw far into the distance, missing scarcely a thing that came within their focusing orbit.

The most outstanding thing about him was by the very nature of it quite unusual. It concerned the texture and colour of his mane and tail. Both were long and flowing, and were of the whitest silver, affording a striking contrast to the rest of him.

Whenever he stood in the shadow of the cliffs, he would be almost invisible but for his mane and tail which seemed to give out a spectral glow.

That he was quick to learn, and becoming more and more accomplished in the art of taking good care of himself, was demonstrated one morning when, with three other colts, they surprised a snake sunnning itself on the flat surface of a rock.

The encounter was made when the colts were stampeding in play up the sandy floor of the canyon that had already witnessed so many of their racing events.

As was usual in these escapades, the Pahute colt was leading by a good four lengths, the warm sand flying up in scattered pa rticles beneath his pounding hooves. He was about half-way up the canyon when an awareness of danger brought him to a stu mbling halt. So sudden was the stop he made that he pra ctically sank back on his buttocks, his forefeet digging into the sand to check the impetus of his muscles.

T he other three colts came stumbling to a halt behind him, all b adly startled when they heard a loud rattling in the near vici nity.

A n instant later, and a huge snake uncurled from the flat-topp ed rock that lay directly in the path of the young horses. The creature's blunt head went up, and then shot out, the fan ged tongue stabbing viciously in the direction of the startled an imals.

The horses rolled their eyes with alarm, all four trembling violently.

With a further harsh rattling in its throat, the snake uncoiled still farther, and slid ominously from the rock, its head continuing to dart forward.

The Pahute colt sprang to one side as once again did the snake shoot out its tongue in his direction.

Another second, and there was a shrill, high-pitched neigh, not so much of fear as of anger. It echoed up the canyon, and seemed caught by the northern cliffs and hurled back again. Before the first echo had reached him, the Pahute colt had reared suddenly and brought his forefeet down on the reptile's sliding shape. Yet again did the colt leap, twisting his body first one way then another, and again did his hooves beat down upon the now writhing coils of the snake.

Then as quickly as it had begun, the attack was over, the Pahute colt leaping a full ten feet from the writhing, threshing coils, while the other three animals turned about and went racing back to the security of Red River Canyon.

Before their companion could follow them, the snake, ra ttling loudly, went sliding under the rock.

The young horse stood for a second trembling, with the sweat of fear making dank the sheen of his hide. Then he too was off, racing with streaming tail after the others, the whites of his eyes disclosing the terror that drove him forward, fleeter than the wind in storm, and never once deviating from a straight course down the canyon.

CHAPTER FIVE

THERE was, on the eastern slopes of the Pine Forest Mountains, a very narrow divide that fell steeply to an enclosed river basin situated between the main escarpment and a more easterly spur.

It was certainly a route into Red River Canyon, but not even the most adventurous of old-timers would have been attracted by it. Not only was it exceedingly dangerous, but it rose tortuously over terrain that was broken into many small ravines that were of volcanic origin. Moreover, the actual gully-track to the divide was a dark-walled portal striking into the living rock. None but a four-footed creature could have attempted any entrance into the canyon by such a devious route.

None did save an albino stallion and his yearling son.

The pair came up into the enclosed river basin by way of the Quinn River, travelling down off the Jackson Mountains into the dreaded Black Rock Desert. Once there, they were not long in leaving the inhospitable desert Badlands. They encountered the river at the point where the eastern spur of the Pine Forest range seemed more inviting than the territory adjacent to Quinn River Crossing in the north-east.

In less than a week, both horses found themselves in the neighbourhood of tough grassland that was to support them for the short period of their stay.

The Albino, some four years old, was restless.

Having lost the one mare he had acquired to a more experienced stallion, he now sought to acquire others so that he could be leader of a herd. His restlessness constantly urged him to leave the grassland and travel on, and at the beginning of the third week, he showed every inclination to follow the

34

inland river to the mountain barrier that supported the canyons on the western slopes of the Pine Forest range.

The instant he betrayed this eagerness to continue the long and arduous trek, the younger animal encouraged him by his display of excitement. It was clear that he was fully prepared to go wherever his sire chose to lead.

For the next few days, both animals moved deeper and deeper into the desolation of ravines and volcanic outcrops. Each day brought nearer the eastern walls of the mountain range, the pitted bulwarks supporting the high peaks appearing, from the river basin, not only formidable, but completely unscalable.

Then one evening at sunset the streaming of the afterglow through the divide, told the Albino that his trail to the wild horse canyons lay over the pass.

He and the yearling pressed on with renewed confidence.

It was almost a week before the two animals reached the divide.

Once over the pass the white stallion knew that before him, was good grazing country. As he stood peering across the array of cliffs and canyons, his nostrils flared, and he began testing every current of air that came to him. Suddenly he was moved to great excitement. He whinnied. He scented mares a-plenty. The yearling also, expressed unusual interest in the scents carried on the air streams.

That same day, the two horses moved down the trail in the direction of the Red Canyon country, heading unerringly towards Red River Valley and Blue Streak's herd of mares. . . .

*　　*　　*　　*　　*

A pair of eagles rising suddenly from the ridge alerted the Pahute colt.

His eyes followed the encircling flight of the birds. Then he saw them suddenly dive with wings partially closed. At the same time, the eagles started to call out, one to the other, and swinging about, followed a spiral of air that took them up over the pass. They seemed to lean on the wind currents for a few moments, then with a warning call, went gliding over the ridge, and vanished.

A second later, the Albino and his yearling son came startlingly into view, both etched against the skyline.

The Pahute colt trembled. He sensed that the strangers had been the cause of the eagles' hasty glide up the mountain. Even though the horses were too far away for the colt to have any direct impression of them, he knew them for what they were, and he instantly faced the canyon and sent a long, whinneying cry resounding down the hillside.

Again and yet again did he send the call until at last Blue Streak ranging the lower end of Red River Canyon, was drawn to the repeated echoes that seemed to fill the canyon with sound.

He became suspicious, recognising the voice as one from his own herd. Pawing the ground with annoyance, he felt compelled to listen. There was a vibrating insistence in the call that spoke clearly of impending danger.

Blue Streak held his head high. As he tested the air currents, he bristled instantly, understanding at last the reason for the call.

Whinneying with suppressed anger, he galloped up the canyon. He had no definite approach point in mind, relying entirely upon the taint in the wind to guide him.

Swiftly, and with deadly intent, he went snaking past the mares scattered half-way up the valley. Then, hearing once again the call from the eastern bulwarks of the canyon, he stopped abruptly.

One quick glance gave him sight of the Pahute colt. On the opposite side of the ravine, he beheld the shape of the Albino stallion, and his companion.

Meanwhile, the white horse and the yearling had reached a

ledge that ran from east to west of the narrow trail they had followed. They paused, with only the deeply shelving ravine separating them from the Pahute colt.

Red River Canyon lay like a chequered map below, and both animals from such a vantage point had no difficulty whatever in seeing right down the watercourse to the widening valley beyond that contained the monuments. They could discern also the far-off lower valley that, had they but known it, was an easier route to the eastern approaches of the Quinn River.

Most important of all, they could see the several scattered groups of mares that made up Blue Streak's herd.

This apparent calm of the entire herd had a stimulating effect on the Albino. He had no distrust in what he saw, and therefore no premonition of danger. The mares for the most part presented no problem as far as he could determine. His main objective would be in the isolated groups nearest the point where the trail from the divide ended in a small hollow. These mares all seemed young, and would be easily enticed away from the main herd.

The Albino snorted with satisfaction, as he set off down the trail, the younger horse hesitating for some minutes before deciding to follow him.

Unlike his sire, the yearling was keenly aware of the danger that would overtake them both the instant they started to round up the mares.

The fear he felt, walked with him; nor did it diminish when he became suddenly aware of the Pahute colt on the other side of the ravine, also picking his way down towards the floor of the valley.

For half an hour or more, Blue Streak stood watching every step the Albino took. Once, and once only, did he send a hard, brassy call resounding up the hillside.

At last he could see the white shape of the invading stallion no longer . . . only the more cautious movement of the younger horse who still had some distance to travel before reaching the floor of the canyon.

Blue Streak's ears went forward. His nostrils opened wide. One further glance he gave to the yearling, and from him, his gaze travelled to the ledge where the Pahute colt had been. The colt was no longer within sight. He had left his vantage point to be in the canyon to join in the affray he sensed would come.

The high wind from the north was unfurling the clouds over the distant Strident Peak on the Nevada—Oregon State Line. Soon they were scattering like tattered pennants all over the Pine Forest range. Then just as the interplay of sunshine and shadow went racing over Red River Canyon, the Albino stallion from the Jackson Mountains came up out of the hollow to round up the mares.

At the same instant, the younger horse came off the mountain trail only to find himself face to face with the Pahute colt. The next moment and both were engaged in a struggle for mastery. Five seconds later the Albino and Blue Streak were preparing to do battle!

The canyon, in that split second of time, so important in the lives of the mares, and doubly so in the life of the Albino, became a fighting centre of startling ferocity.

As the white stallion approached the first of the herd, Blue Streak whirled around, lifted his head and uttered his anger cry. He plunged forward, thrusting in amongst the mares at a gallop. He weaved in and out of the band, swung half-right and then attacked the Albino side-on.

The Albino saw the danger that threatened. His back arched and his head went up as Blue Streak drove in on him. He was lifted clean off his feet, and although winded by the attack, was yet as quick as his opponent. As the black stallion whirled up to bring his forelegs down on him, the Albino, following the old and well-tried trick adopted by wild animals in adversity, rolled completely over. He was on his legs in a trice, and went in to the attack. Kicking and plunging, his lips drawn back in a vicious snarl, he made a determined effort to rip Blue Streak from rump to belly.

By now, the entire canyon was echoing to the shrill screams of conflict and the terrified pounding of hooves as the herd went racing away from the wrestling stallions.

The conflict was no less bitter where the Pahute colt and the yearling were at grips. Although neither had the experience of the other two stallions, what they lacked in knowledgeable strategy they made up in sheer brute force.

Both were leaping, kicking, and biting; moreover, both had succeeded in drawing blood. The advantages, however, were clearly with the Pahute colt. His additional height and weight gave him a decisive body-breaking power over his opponent. Meanwhile, farther over in the battle arena, Blue Streak had got the Albino confused. He gave a trumpeting cry of savage ecstacy as his head went down, then up, his jaws opening wide, his teeth clicking menacingly as he sought the other's throat. Although he missed the hold he had hoped to get, Blue Streak brought a gush of blood pouring down the Albino's chest where he had opened up a large wound.

No pause was there in the attack despite this unexpected achievement. The white stallion seemed in no way disconcerted although he was bleeding profusely.

Blue Streak jumped away from his opponent, seeming to give the other animal a short respite. The Albino stood back, blowing through his nostrils and discharging blood with each gasp. Then, just as he was taking another deep breath, Blue Streak was at him again, this time almost dropping to his knees before swinging up. The black stallion's head forced up the Albino's muzzle. A second later and there was a further tearing of flesh as Blue Streak's teeth made yet another gash. Scarcely another second had passed and Blue Streak was standing on his hind legs, his forelegs locked tightly around the Albino's neck.

39

Backwards and forwards swayed the two stallions, all the advantage with Blue Streak, while the Albino's hooves tore into the ground as he tried to get himself into a steady stance.

No matter what he did, his legs seemed unable to give him adequate support. He slithered in the sand until he was almost on his rump.

He twisted and tried to turn from one side to the other, but nothing he did could break the death-locking grip Blue Streak had on his neck.

The wide opening of the Albino's nostrils told only too clearly of his great distress. His eyes too were full of the terror he felt. Not for much longer could he withstand Blue Streak's agonizing hold. His hind legs failed him. He sank back on his rump, a new surging of fear dimming his vision. Not for nothing that sense of fear! He saw the end all too distinctly despite the dimming of vision.

Suddenly, the hold Blue Streak had on him was loosened. He opened his jaws to draw air into his lungs. Before he could do so, or make any attempt to protect himself, all the dreams he had of possessing some of Blue Streak's mares went out in a blinding flash of pain.

A faint sound reached his ears. . . . He could not identify it! What he could identify, however, was the distorted shape rearing above him. Then it was all over. Blue Streak's right hoof shattered his skull, and with that blow went the last of the Albino's hearing . . . the last of his sight. No more for him the mountains and the streams . . . the lush grassland in winter and the hill shadows in summer.

All were gone, taken away in one blow from a stallion who had never known defeat from another of his kind.

Only the cloud shapes raced like a phantom herd across the floor of the canyon where the Albino stretched out in his last sleep. Then, echoing from cliff to cliff, resounded Blue Streak's awesome scream of triumph.

The yearling heard it as he went scrambling in terror up the

trail to the divide, having himself only escaped death by a
hair's breadth when he had broken free from the Pahute colt
and confused him by galloping off before he could recover
from the surprise he had experienced.

Again and yet again did Blue Streak's call of triumph reach
up to him from out of the canyon now full of racing shadows.

CHAPTER SIX

Next day was one of uncertainty for the herd grazing in Red River Canyon. None of the mares showed any inclination to penetrate that corner of the valley where the white stallion lay motionless. The only sign of movement came from the constantly wheeling vultures who, having come from all points of the mountain range, yet lacked sufficient courage to alight in the canyon and begin their grim feasting. They, like the mares, feared the ceaseless prowling of the huge black stallion.

Most of the young stallions—many of them little more than well-grown yearlings—also kept well out of the way of their sire. Among them was the Pahute colt. He had walked warily up the canyon the previous night, and sensing by the distant trumpetings that Blue Streak was still angry despite his victory over the Albino, he had gone to a small creak coming down direct from the hills on the north side of the valley, the small stream it contained emptying itself into the Red River.

❦　　❦　　❦　　❦　　❦

It was a little before sunset before Blue Streak entered the creek. All afternoon he had paced around the herd, seeking out the yearling stallions he had suddenly decided to eject and drive away. Times there were when the young horses stood away off in groups, and made no attempt to scatter until their sire came at them in anger.

The great stallion had no sooner headed into the approaches of the creek when he glimpsed the Pahute colt, and discerned that the yearlings he had cut out from the band were already showing the young horse a measure of obedience. They stood in a rough semi-circle around him, the colt himself, distinctive by his silver mane and tail, standing a little in advance of the others, looking direct at his sire. There was, moreover, something in his stance that savoured of defiance.

Blue Streak bristled. Everything he beheld in that moment of rising anger was too much of an old familiar pattern to warrant leniency on his part. Even so, despite this knowledge so strongly manifest in the swift running of his blood, he stood for a while longer, gazing at the colt. The stallion then felt welling up in him something that was more of his youth than of the present.

He ceased to bristle, and looking past the colt, glanced up the creek. He knew this place very well. He had been in it many times before, and once had travelled far up the narrow canyon into the very depths of the mountains. The stream that here, flowed down to the Red River, was a tributary from a much larger watercourse far in the fold of the hills—the Yellow River, the Indians called it.

Blue Streak who had investigated it carefully, had followed the waterway many miles into the mountains until he reached the awesome place amidst the crags where it fell, seething and shrieking, into one of the enormous sinks that swallowed so many rivers in Nevada and Idaho.

A movement from those yearlings encircling the Pahute colt drew the stallion's attention once again to the matter that had, till this brief excursion into the past, occupied all his time since early morning.

He interpreted the slow forward step the colt took in his direction as a prelude to a general stampede to break out from the creek.

The stallion, without further hesitation, threw up his head and pawed the ground. He then uttered a savage scream, and even while it was yet issuing from his wide-flung jaws, all the young horses, still smarting from his recent attacks on them, turned tail and were racing in a flurry of blacks, roans and reds up the steeply rising floor of the creek.

Only one remained—the Pahute colt! Fraught though the moment was with suspense and possible danger, the young horse had stood his ground.

Blue Streak, beholding him as one who challenged him, tensed his muscles to take action. In the very second of his intended assault, there seemed to rise up before him a vision that checked all instinctive movement.

The black stallion snorted angrily, distrusting anything he could not understand. Despite the overwhelming desire to go into the attack, he yet made no move to overthrow the colt.

The vision had become clearer in his eyes. It grew until Blue Streak saw not the deep cleft in the Pine Forest Mountains, but an alkali mud flat far back in Southern Nevada, and beyond it, a scrub-topped hill and a narrow valley lying between it and another hill of similar shape and size.

Around the mud flat he seemed to glimpse horses . . . many of them. In the narrow valley between the two hills, he saw just one horse . . . an animal very young . . . one obviously just cut out from the herd and now denied the right to drink from the pool east of the mud flat.

That young stallion stood as the Pahute colt was now standing, daring any other animal to invade the canyon, yet, at the same time, afraid to leave it to seek water. . . .

Then Blue Streak, the great stallion from the arid mountains of Nevada, understood the meaning of the vision. In looking at the Pahute colt, he was looking at himself in the years that had gone . . . himself and none other. The Pahute colt was but a manifestation of that past, and was the very embodiment of Blue Streak save for the silver mane and tail.

*　　　*　　　*　　　*　　　*

The Pahute colt was sensitively aware of some change come over his sire. He knew that the stallion desired him no harm.

At the same time, he sensed that Blue Streak did not intend that he should rejoin the herd.

Then the colt interpreted in the singing of his blood what Blue Streak sought to tell him. He received the knowledge with a sense of rapture.

His sire was giving him freedom from the bondage of obedience. He was, in addition, imparting to him all that he himself had known in the past . . . the story of the winds and the rushing rivers . . . the beauty of the prairies in moonlight and the long, winding trails when the night was gone and the new day about to dawn . . . the blue brightness of the mountains in summer and the darkness that stood over them when the whirlwinds came.

One deep sigh came from the colt's very heart, and with it, ebbed the last of the animosity he felt. He remembered only that not many hours since he had fought as much for Blue Streak as for himself.

He tossed his head, and his mane rippled like a torrent of silver pouring over his arched neck.

For perhaps a second longer he stood looking at Blue Streak. Then, without haste, or fear, he turned away, and went at a slow gallop after those others who were making their way towards the Yellow River set in the grip of the mountains.

*   *   *   *   *

The black stallion lifted his head, the better to watch the colt making his unhurried journey up into the hills. Then he made the mountains resound with his clarion call of farewell. Never before had he sent a colt away from the herd with such a bugle note of goodwill; but then, never before had he recognized so clearly in a colt his own blood, and the blood of Diablo, the Apache devil horse.

Not long afterwards, Blue Streak returned quietly to the herd in Red River Canyon.

Book Two
Horse of the West Wind

CHAPTER SEVEN

TIME in the great world of the wild was recognized only by the changing seasons which, in their turn, brought change to the habits of those who dwelt in the wilderness. Thus a full year passed quickly by and the yearling stallion Blue Streak had sent away from the herd in Red River Canyon became in very truth an animal of great power and beauty.

Apart from the fact that he stood high in the leg in contrast to the average mustang, he also possessed a remarkably broad and open chest, denoting good heart room, which no doubt, accounted for his great speed in running.

His colour, however, during that year, had changed but little, save that perhaps it was now a deeper black and the silver mane and tail more lustrous in texture, and almost white. For the rest, he was as distinctive a horse as any that could be found in either Nevada, Oregon or Idaho. Moreover, he was a lone ranger, having no intimate companions and, for the moment, not conscious of any desire to inherit a herd of his own.

He ranged for the most part between the easterly foothills of the Pine Forest Mountains and the Quinn River. He had, in that first year of freedom, penetrated into the mountain fastnesses bounded by Trident Peak on the Nevada—Oregon State Line and Split Peak farther south; but always, when on such expeditions, some obscure instinct brought him back south to the Quinn River until at last he recognized it as his own special grazing territory, and seldom went far from it.

In the first place, the grazing was as good as any he had found elsewhere, in the second place, never in all that year of wandering, had he seen anything to cause him apprehension. It seemed that man, the hunter of his kind, seldom came to this hinterland of mountain, desert and river.

More than anything else in the whole world, the stallion loved running great distances, his long legs moving tirelessly, his entire body responding to the mysterious pulse of life within him. It was this acute awareness of life beating strong in him that so often urged him to gallop and gallop until the unattainable horizon had dwindled as it always did to either a mountain outcrop, or to great coloured reaches of desert, with a distant bench of fantastic rock as formidable as any mountain cliff, and as equally difficult to explore.

That the stallion did explore many of these benches, and successfully too, gave him a sureness of foot that, in the years to come, was to confound many who sought to catch him.

One such bench of spiral-like mountain lay at the southern toe of the eastern foothills of the Pine Forest range. It attracted the young stallion more than any other place he knew.

When he first glimpsed it, wonder and awe stimulated his appetite for exploration. It was like a menace flung at him that, at the same time, urged him to penetrate and subdue whatever mystery it might contain. The massive, spiralling outcrop, rose in a series of ledges from the yellow valley of the desert.

Some thirty odd miles to the south-east, ran the Quinn River. From the watercourse, seeming a great distance away, the queer pinnacled mountain was as enticing as it was forbidding.

Many times when grazing along the shore of the river, the stallion would raise his head and stare for a long time across the ribbed sand-dunes. Always was his gaze drawn to the far-off tower of rock, but he never visited it until the memorable day when a whirlwind came shrieking over the Black Rock Desert.

There was a wild wailing in the air when the stallion quitted the river pasture where he had been for some days, and he was half-way across the desert with the bench still a good couple of hour's steady pacing away when the wailing increased.

The horse beheld the ominous whirling cloud of sand

approaching. Scrub and dwarfed trees seemed caught up in
the vast maw of the vortex that assumed the shape of the
mountain bench the stallion was intent on reaching.

Neighing with fear, he started to run, soon outpacing the
whirling column of sand. His white stockings winked as he
ran, his long neck thrust out to its fullest extent.

With each step he took, the horizon-wide face of the bench
came steadily nearer. Like an advance guard of the sand
column, four eagles went swooping overhead, making for the
same refuge as the stallion. The birds were over the racing
horse, then lost in the rising pancake-shape of the bench in
as many paces as it took the stallion to cover a dozen yards.

By this time, the Pahute stallion was possessed with but one
aim—to reach the mountainous outcrop before he was caught
up in the whirling curtain of sand.

Like an ocean, smoothed out and quietened, the last of the
sand dunes gave way to a carpet of untrodden yellow, and
standing at the very edge of it, ribbed and scalloped, rose the
first of the pancake-shaped benches.

The wail of the whirlwind was now a shrieking of many
voices, and with a wild snort, the stallion charged—a black
fury of leaping heels and tossing mane into the mouth of the
first canyon. He soon found himself in a maze of encircling
trails, all leading upwards, some ending on small mesas, others
twisting up higher still to the topmost pancake spread of rock
that was a veritable spire of an ancient desert cathedral
fashioned by a million, million years of unhurried time.

In the first surge of rising fear that drove him far into the
canyon that offered him protection from the whirlwind, the
stallion noticed nothing peculiar about the outcrop of mountain.

When, at last, the whirlwind passed away northwards,
having been torn free of the mountain by contrary currents of
air, the horse became aware of a silence that was like the
hidden pounding of his own heart . . . deep, brooding, and
mysterious. . . .

He stood for a very long time indeed listening to it, before he began to work the nearest trail, travelling up and up as if on a spiral staircase. In places, the walls were barely fifty feet apart, in others, as wide as two hundred feet.

Many of the benches that afforded him a brief breathing space were heavy in gloom while others were bright and hot with sunshine. More than ever, in his climbing, was he like a ghost horse . . . almost invisible save for his mane and tail when the benches were steeped in heavy shadow, then startlingly alive and magnificently poised when he came full into the sunshine, to stare down upon the now undisturbed sweep of the desert and the distant Quinn River with its twin loops adjacent to the Jackson Mountains and the Black Rock Desert.

Finally, he rested in the harsh glare of the sunshine on the highest of the pancake benches which was but a caprock of some hundred feet in extent, without any break in it, and almost as smooth as glass.

He could reach no higher!

*   *   *   *   *

All around lay the vast uncompromising world of desert and mountain, the land-locked river between the foothills and the Pine Forest range seeming little more than a glint of silver in the awesome wilderness of volcanic canyons and seamed rock faces.

Directly below the caprock, was the largest of the huge benches, and south of it, the buttress that supported the plateau, fell steeply two thousand feet or more to the boulder-strewn valley of the land-locked river.

He uttered, as Blue Streak so often did, his scream of triumph that echoed far out into the desert. Maybe it was carried on an air stream as far as the Quinn River, for a solitary horseman paused and listened, and wondered if it was the voice of the whirlwind . . . returning. . . .

49

CHAPTER EIGHT

THE horseman, Jim Blaine, was, at the time of the whirlwind, on the wrong side of the Quinn River. He was a young man of about twenty-four or five, lean, but well set, and with muscles that were typical of a young fellow who used his body for work which he enjoyed. Inclined to fairness, his skin was freckled in places where it was not too deeply tanned by exposure to the sun.

His father, Jeff Blaine, was a rancher whose main activity centred around horses and cattle. He had set up camp a few miles east of the Quinn River Crossing—a ford that gave the only safe passage from one bank to the other, intent in surveying the surrounding country for possible grazing for a new herd of cattle he was bent on bringing in from the east.

Jim had other ideas. He was ambitious, his head full of the many tales he had heard from time to time of the great herds of wild horses that ranged the western territories of the Pine Forest Mountains. It was while trying to pick up some trace of wild horses that he found himself in his unenviable position when the whirlwind came up.

He immediately set about finding shelter. Only one place seemed likely—an outcrop of rocks. Then with his horse well protected in an acclivity beside him, he resigned himself to sit out the dust storm.

It was not until the whirlwind vanished northwards that Jim Blaine found his attention focused on that queer pancake-shape that stood out from the main spread of mountain that broke the western skyline.

As he remounted his horse and prepared to cross the river for the homeward trek, he felt a warm burst of wind sweeping across the desert. A few scattered whorls of sand marked its course which seemed to be direct from the pancake mountain. Then as the wind blew over a little more strongly, he sat up taut in the saddle, as he caught some queer sound in the air currents.

For a moment he scanned the northern horizon, thinking that it was the whirlwind returning. Then, since the horizon was clear of dust clouds, he half-leant into the wind as if to drag from it some clue as to the nature of the cry he thought he could still hear.

He listened intently. It was a sound like a scream . . . the scream, surely, of some animal or other. . . .

Although nothing moved in all that sweep of desert save the whorls of dust whipped by the breeze, the scream, if indeed he was not being deceived, was something that came from way out beyond the dust . . . something that surely emanated from the pancake mountain bench that now stood revealed more clearly than ever.

The young man was intrigued as never before. Here was something as mysterious as the desert and the mountain bench. He shaded his eyes with one hand over his brow and continued to gaze at the fantastic array of rocks. The sound, if sound there was, had gone with the last burst of wind, and there was only a silence. . . .

He resolved there and then to explore the strange rock formation the very next day.

Jeff Blaine listened to his son's story that evening with scepticism.

'There ain't nothin' much out in that bit o' desert save coyotes, Jimmie boy,' Blaine said at last. 'As any old-timer will tell you, the Black Rock Desert ain't the place where a man can get off the trail, an' live. No sir! There's sulphur out there that would stifle you before you were a day out. . . .' Then nodding his head as if with some secret knowledge of the desert nobody else possessed, he added: 'I ain't never heard of cattle or hosses livin' out there. Only the coyotes. . . .'

It was then that one of the cattlemen—a thick-set, bearded individual—made the only interesting comment, at least, as far as Jimmie was concerned.

'They do say,' he remarked thoughtfully, looking full at the young man, 'that over in the mountains of the west are the best of the wild hoss herds this side of Idaho an' Utah. Even so, it's as the boss says . . . that's a long way off beyond the desert . . . a very long way. . . .'

'Then it's no idle talk about there being wild hosses out there in the west?' Jim asked, with renewed interest.

The cattleman shook his head.

'There's wild hosses a-plenty. Good hosses too, some of them are from all accounts, but no man has ever crossed that desert to my knowledge an' returned to tell whether or not he himself has seen them. . . .'

He paused, looking at young Blaine in a way that was calculated to make him even more curious.

'Then how can you be so sure?' Jim asked, to the cattleman's deep satisfaction.

The fellow sighed, and shrugged his shoulders.

'Just tales I've heard . . . always tales, an' few of them differing one from the other.' He leant forward, poking Jimmie in the ribs. '. . . wild hosses a-plenty, an' all led by some big stallion or other. One hoss was seen by a Paiute Indian named Roki. A blue-black hoss way up in the Wind River Mountains. Trailed him up a gulch until he lost him. The stallion just vanished, an' from all accounts, he ain't never showed up since. . . .'

'Ain't never?' queried the other cattleman.

'Well, there's the tales about the hoss, Blue Streak.'

'That's the hoss I'm recalling to mind.'

Young Blaine looked from one man to the other.

'Who is Blue Streak?' he asked eagerly.

His father patted him on the shoulder, and laughed.

'Just another of them great hosses everybody has seen at

some time or another, but ain't never caught. Anyways, one thing you can be sure about . . . the desert ain't Blue Streak's ranging territory. . . .'

'Maybe,' said Jim. 'Maybe not.'

*   *   *   *   *

Jim Blaine was awake early next morning. Just as the dawn came stealing across the distant Santa Rosa Mountains, he quitted his bed and prepared the camp-fire for breakfast.

His father and the bearded cowman joined him. Both men exchanged glances at Jim's early rising.

'Figuring on going some place, Jim?' the elder Blaine asked.

'Yep. I kinda thought of going across the river again and making for the bench way out in the desert. . . .'

'Wild Hoss Bench!' the cowman remarked drily.

Jim Blaine's head shot up at that.

'Do you mean there *are* wild hosses there?'

The cowman shook his head emphatically.

'Nope! Not any more. It's as your father said last night. There's no hosses this side of the Pine Forest range. As fer Wild Hoss Bench, there was a tale a long while back about a stallion called Starface from No Man's Land over in the Cimarron River area. He was said to have taken refuge fer a bit on Wild Hoss Bench.'

The elder Blaine appeared most interested in all the cowman said.

*   *   *   *   *

But an hour later, young Blaine and the cowman called Jake were heading for Quinn River Crossing and the desert Badlands that stretched away from the watercourse to the pancake-shaped mountain known as 'Wild Hoss Bench'!

They halted that evening in a bend of the river basin, setting up camp on what appeared to be excellent grazing ground.

Their horses, hobbled against straying, appeared content to remain near the river bank.

It was not long before Jim discovered some horse droppings. He stared at them for a few seconds, then shouted for his companion.

The cowman stood in silence for a moment or two, then said slowly and a trifle reflectively: 'There's been a hoss here sure enough. Sure you wasn't here yourself yesterday?'

Blaine shook his head emphatically.

'Then it can only be a wild hoss. . . . There ain't nothin' else hereabouts unless it be some prospector's mustang that's become a stray which ain't at all likely. . . .' He stared for a moment out into the desert, then turned his gaze northwards. Scratching his head as if perplexed, he said softly, more to himself than to his companion: 'Wonder if it's Blue Streak back from across the State Line? . . . .'

'Could be, if what you've said about that hoss is right,' Jimmie replied.

The cowman did not answer immediately, but continued to gaze away to the north. He then said abruptly 'We'll make for the bench soon after sun-up. We'll visit Wild Hoss Bench an' find out.'

Before they turned in for the night, both men could not resist staring across the desert Badlands to the distant mountain. They saw the groined buttress walls quite clearly for a few minutes, as if the evening light had brought an expected clarity to the desert. They saw too the main bench about five hundred feet up, and rising way above it, in a series of whorls and pinnacles, the pancake formation of immense outcrops piled one on top of the other. They appeared dark and threatening as the light seemed suspended over them.

Clearly also was revealed the topmost spread of rock . . . the final pinnacle. Then like a mysterious hand drawing a veil over the fantastic up-thrust of mountain, the light went retreating over the mountains of the west and the painted desert.

At last, the horizon was no more than varying shadows among deeper shadows that hid whatever might lay out there in the west.

The cowman yawned.

'This is sure a good place to camp. There's grass, water, an' a bit of driftwood for the fire. We couldn't hev done better.'

'Yep,' Jim murmured, still staring out into the fast gathering gloom of night.

Then, as often happened in the desert Badlands of the west, one flickering glow of light spread for an instant over the skyline. The far end of Wild Hoss Bench stood out for a second in supreme isolation. It was as though a beacon had been kindled in the sky.

Another moment, and the glow went dying down the corridors of the mountains, and it was night in the desert, and over the broken towers of Wild Hoss Bench. . . .

CHAPTER NINE

Next morning, in the sharp, cold light of dawn, both men moved quietly about the camp, Jimmie preparing the fire so that he could cook breakfast, while Jake went down to the river to wash.

As Jim squatted back on his heels watching the smoke rise into the air, he wondered what the day was going to bring forth. Was he expecting too much from Jake's casual remarks that the only horse known to have visited Wild Hoss Bench was a stallion as famous as any that roamed Nevada?

He did not know what to think. It all seemed so utterly impossible, and yet, there was the evidence of the droppings! Some horse or other had certainly been over to the river. Possibly he had come only for water. . . . Nothing else! Even so, such an animal had done what Jeff Blaine said no horse was likely to do—had come down either from Wild Hoss Bench or from some other place far north. What was more important, he had been here . . . almost in this very spot. . . .

His thoughts broke off as he heard Jake shouting. Rising to his feet, he looked towards the river bank. The cowman was waving his arms.

Jim started to run, and when within a few yards of Jake, he stopped, staring down. There, leading to the river's edge, were hoof marks—not the iron-shod marks of a saddle horse, but the horn marks of an animal that had never submitted to the indignity of a shaped shoe and nail.

Jake was beside himself with excitement.

'It's no ordinary beast,' he began. 'You can tell by the size of them prints. The hoss that made them must be big . . . very big! See how they are paced? They'm wider apart than the mustang an' more firmly set in the sand. . . .'

He paused for a moment, scratching in his beard. Then in ill-disguised excitement, he declared: 'It's Blue Streak, without a doubt. If it ain't him, it's another like him. . . .' 'We'll hit the trail to Wild Hoss Bench. Mebbe it's there we'll find the hoss that made them hoof marks.'

Both men then hurried back to camp, and in less than an hour, were riding out into the desert, heading for the pancake mountain over in the west.

*   *   *   *   *

The afternoon was well advanced when Blaine and the cowman topped the last ridge and reining in their horses, gazed down upon the last couple of miles to Wild Hoss Bench.

Before them were partial washes and dips where water might have lodged in times of heavy rain. There was also the only resemblance of a trail the men had seen since leaving the Quinn River. Jake, gazing down upon it, likened it in his mind to a tortuous passage rather than any trail made by man and beast. No spearhead of grass grew in the washes, no sagebrush in the dips, and the trail, such as it was, slipped past like a faint shadow, but a shadow which, none the less, led direct to the mountain and the first canyon mouth that yawned ominously and spilled its accumulation of rubbish on to the carpet of untrodden sand before it.

His face wore a puzzled frown. Somewhere, in the deeps of his mind, stirred some vague memory of a place seen or the echo of words spoken, describing it.

In silence, both men rode over towards the ribbed and scalloped buttress wall supporting the bench. Minutes later they made another startling discovery. They discerned more hoof marks, and saw that they came in at a point a little north of the route they themselves had taken from the river.

Jake uttered a sharp exclamation at sight of the hoof marks, and the great stretch of yellow sand which was so utterly different from the washes and dips of the route they had followed.

He halted his horse and glanced back along the trail. His brow was puckered as he sought once again to unravel the problem that lay deep in his mind . . . a problem surely that had its being in some chance remark made years before about the Black Rock Desert and an area of red water washes before a 'haunted hoss bench'.

Turning to his companion, he exclaimed: 'I've been wonderin' what was familiar about that trail we followed through the dips an' washes. It ain't that I've been here ever, but I seem to recall some other place like it, mebbe, only there ain't no such place. Now I know why I remembered. . . .'

He paused and Jim looked at him inquiringly.

'Well?' he asked softly.

'It was described to me by old Colorado Ted,' Jake resumed. 'In fact, it was amongst them same washes an' dips that Ted once saw Blue Streak. He described him as "a great blue-black hoss standin' high in the leg. . . . A bold hoss . . . an' vicious." Ted remarked that when he drew close, the stallion pawed the ground, then he wuz away like a dark flame. . . . That's what Ted said. . . . "A dark flame!" ' he sighed heavily.

'Them hoof marks . . . they ain't Blue Streak's. He'd have come in by the old trail the same as we did. They belong to some other hoss.'

'But it could be Blue Streak who made the hoof marks in the sand. . . . Blue Streak come back from the north where he he had been driven by the ranchers from the Indian Creek country,' Jim reasoned, determined to hang on to his hopes.

He stared hard and long at the cathedral-like mountain before him. The scalloped walls, the rising benches, and that topcap rock so high above the outer pinnacles, possessed an even stranger fascination. He felt the breath choking in his throat and a quickening in his heart-beat as his eyes narrowed perceptibly to focus the more clearly on that summit ledge.

Then he gave a cry, pointing upwards.

Something was indeed standing on that topcap rock a full four thousand feet above the desert. The figure, however, was so small that it could not easily be identified, and moreover, the head was not set in the direction of the Quinn River, but due west.

'It's a hoss!' Jake exclaimed.

Jimmie was puzzled.

'I'm not so sure,' he replied at last. 'It just don't seem real to me.'

'Watch!' the other murmured. 'Just watch!'

What happened next engraved itself on the men's memories for all time. The diminutive figure reared. It pawed the air.

As if to dispel the last of their doubts, both men heard what Jim alone had heard once before on the wind . . . a scream that could now be identified as the call of a stallion. . . .

The scream remained in their ears long after the shape of the horse on the Caprock had gone.

*　　*　　*　　*　　*

Jim and Jake rested awhile under the buttressed walls of the bench. They had a meal and discussed their next move. Since it would soon be nightfall, they had no choice for the present but to set up camp and investigate the interior canyons of the mountain next day.

Both men fretted at the enforced delay, but it was obvious that very little would be gained by pressing on until next morning. As Jake remarked, there was always another day, and to proceed in darkness might well end in disaster.

They slept ill that night. Even their horses seemed unduly restless. The first glimmer of dawn was making a tracery of colour in the east when one of the horses neighed. But the men did not wake, and even the chipmunk that looked out from under a pile of rocks, blinked at the gloom and went back to sleep.

Dawn seemed a long time coming despite the gathering of light on the eastern horizon, but by the time the stars were fading, Jimmie and Jake were up and about, and before sun-up, were saddling their horses.

A queer, half-gloom still hovered in the main canyon when they rode through the gap in the mountain walls. It gave an added mystery to the scene. The very instant they reined their horses to a halt to peer about them, they became aware of the awesome silence that brought an unexpected chill to their spines. Neither of the men had known anything like it before. They looked at each other, unwilling to speak lest their voices intruded on something that, throughout the long years, had never heard the sound of human speech.

Then the cowman pointed to the nearest trail that went up and up like a spiral staircase. He still did not speak, but Jim interpreting his wishes, nodded his head in agreement.

They moved at a slow pace, their horses at first reluctant to set foot on such a hazardous trail, and then, as they were encouraged by softly uttered words of command, setting their feet more firmly on the track and going up with a sign of greater assurance in their gait.

'Do you think we might see the stallion?' Jimmie asked at last, speaking quietly.

His companion shrugged his shoulders.

'Mebbe,' he replied, 'especially if this is the only trail to them higher benches.'

His tones were quietly pitched, matching Jim's own.

Further comment was rendered impossible since the trail narrowed considerably and the rock walls were closing in to such an extent that the two riders felt they were entering a tunnel carved out in the mountain. In a little while, however, they came out on to the first of the benches, and one that faced westwards to the Pine Forest Mountains across the valley.

The cowman who was in the lead reined in his horse. Turning to Jimmie, he said with disappointment: 'As far as the stallion is concerned, we need go no farther. The hoss is away out in the foothills below.'

He indicated the vast world of mountain and the land-locked river in the eastern valley of the Pine Forest range. A single speck moved up in the direction of the volcanic canyons . . . a speck that, after much concentration by Jim, turned out to be a horse.

'It's the stallion all right,' Jake said, this time with emphasis. 'Ain't no other. There's likely another way out of Wild Hoss Bench on the western side.'

'Can't we follow?' Jim asked breathlessly.

The other shook his head emphatically.

'Wouldn't do much good, lad. That hoss would be well up in the hills before we make the river basin, an' looking down on that valley from here, seems to me we'd never get far without extra food. . . .'

Blaine knew that his friend was right. They were quite clearly ill-equipped to penetrate into such a mountain fastness as that which he gazed upon below. The disappointment he felt showed plainly on his face.

'Never mind, Jim,' Jake said gently. 'We might try again some other time. One thing's certain. That stallion knows his way around. Yes sir! Mebbe there's a herd some place up in the watershed. Anyways, Jim, over on them western mountains is the fabled wild hoss canyons of Nevada. You're lookin' straight over at the rangin' country of the great wild hoss bands.'

'If we could but make it . . .' Jim said.

'We can't! It would take days . . . even weeks. Besides, judgin' from the spread of that valley below there, it ends in the northern spur of the main range. There ain't no way out. . . .'

'But that hoss down there?'

'He might know a way up over the foothills into the canyon country of the west. We don't!'

With which remark, he looked Jim straight in the eye.

'We'd be plain mad to go on,' he added.

Jim nodded.

They then turned their horses about, and went back down the trail to camp, a little after mid-day, in the canyon that was steeped in silence.

Meanwhile, down in the eastern watershed of the Pine Forest Mountains, the Pahute stallion, unaware that he had at last been observed by man, the betrayer of his kind, pressed on towards the distant river near which, the previous day, he had glimpsed what appeared to be other horses.

His step was firm; his head held high. He was tired of being alone. The time had come for him to get a herd of his own!

Only once did he pause and look back, gazing up at what was now an unfamiliar aspect of Wild Hoss Bench. He then broke the solemn silence of the valley by giving a wild, piercing whistle.

Before the sound had died away, he was again travelling up the watershed.

His career as one of the famous stallions of the west was about to begin!

CHAPTER TEN

THE Pahute stallion reached the area of volcanic waterholes just as the new moon was rising above the eastern foothills. It had been an arduous trek from Wild Horse Bench, as treacherous as any yet encountered. There had been numerous potholes to avoid, and all, for the most part, situated in the most unlikely places. A broken leg in such a wild and desolate spot would result in a slow and agonizing death, with only birds of prey for company.

Even with this knowledge constantly probing him to caution, the young stallion was in no way deterred. He had discovered very early sufficient evidence of other animals to urge him on, and he finally came up on a small bunch of mares who were pawing for the sparse grass that grew on an isolated flat little more than a couple of miles in extent.

It was miserable grazing at the best, but it was, nevertheless, a strip of pasture that had found roothold, and succeeded in growing, in the most austere surroundings.

The pasture was coarse and thick with sour weed, the one green oasis in a region of rock, and from way back in the long history of the mountains, animals large and small, but mostly ragged bands of wild horses, visited it.

The herd of mares disclosed little interest in the appearance of the young stallion. They continued with their grazing, and only viewed him with a measure of suspicion when he finally came amongst them in order to eat.

All of the mares were stragglers from a large herd that had once roamed the locality of Rebel Creek. During a round-up by a strange stallion from the east, a few of them, escaping from the general confusion that followed, made off in the direction of the Quinn River. Led by a mare of great age, they eventually found their way up the volcanic watershed that lay between the main ridge of the Pine Forest Mountains and the easterly spur of hills that terminated in Wild Horse Bench and the Black Rock Desert.

That night, the Pahute stallion moved contentedly amongst the mares as he grazed. He was completely at ease, refreshing himself occasionally by drinking from the ice-cold pools that were abundant where the pasture gave way to a hard rock floor.

The moon faded away in the sky; daybreak was not far off. As the nearby peaks took shape against the van of the sunrise, and the stallion could discern more clearly the slope of the hills about him, he deserted the mares and moved slowly along the lee of the cliffs until he came to a ledge striking upwards. He started to climb until he finally halted at a small divide which was of recent formation. The piled-up debris was fresh, and quite clearly the result of a fall of rock brought about by long weathering conditions. A fissure in the rock-face, some ten feet in width, had opened up an hitherto unknown exit from the volcanic canyon.

As the stallion, moved by curiosity, penetrated the opening, he beheld a sizeable acclivity sloping away at an easy angle, following a seam in the rock. It ran in an almost unbroken line to the deep valley that struck northwards to Trident Peak on the Nevada Oregon State Line.

There was a sharp run of wind coming down from the north, and it came funnelling up the cleft. The stallion's nostrils flared as he sought to read what the wind had to tell. After a few minutes, he continued to move cautiously along the cleft which gradually widened with each mile he travelled until, in the bright harsh light of a new day, he was able to discern an endless wilderness of peaks stretching northward to what seemed a promising country for a band of mares.

Despite the intriguing nature of the trek he had made, the horse had not forgotten the mares back in the mountain enclosure. He had already resolved to take them as his own, but before doing so, he was anxious to discover suitable range territory. He sensed that the pasture within the mountains would not support the band should there be any increase in its numbers.

Thus he pressed on along what was no more than a corridor in the mountain wall, a corridor, however, that continued to widen, and eventually opened out on to a plateau set a full five thousand feet above the vast sweep of country that separated the eastern spur of the Pine Forest range and the rocky, broken escarpment of Split Peak, adjacent to the Oregon border territories.

Evening was now fast gathering in the plain; moreover, a rainstorm was coming up. Clouds were flying high over the distant peaks, and afar off, the sullen rolling of thunder sounded what might have been an ancient Indian tattoo.

The stallion, undaunted, moved towards the edge of the plateau. Peering over, he made out a similar seam in the rock surface that had characterized the mesa on which he had been born.

His reactions were instantaneous. He remembered the terraces that struck up from the desert to the higher reaches of the mesa; he remembered too, most vividly, the mountain lion Blue Streak had slain. More than that, he recalled the trail he and the other colts had traversed when Blue Streak had got the entire herd on the move, prior to the long journey to Red River Canyon.

The stallion started to investigate the prospects of a similar trail striking down to the plain. As he moved backwards and forwards along the lip of the plateau, he did so with the experience of a horse long grown familiar with the terrain in which he lived and which was characteristic of the entire district of mountain and desert that made up this remote part of Nevada.

It was not long before he came upon a ledge falling away

towards the distant plain, and on closer investigation, knew that it could be negotiated without undue risk.

He snorted with excitement and, what was now becoming a familiar attitude of his, he reared up and screamed, pawing the air with vigour.

A little later, he was on his way back to the mountain grazing, traversing now a corridor dark with night. There was no starlight to guide him through its steep ascent, and he had to rely entirely on the sure touch of his forefeet on the rocky trail to avoid disaster where boulders could do him an injury. All the time, echoing eerily through the cleft, the far off peals of thunder told of the storm still thrashing the mountains of the north.

It was almost daybreak before he came again to the inner canyon between the stark, uprising cliffs of mountain, and saw, mis-shapen in the slow gathering light, the shapes of mares, grazing. . . .

The Pahute stallion reared and uttered a challenging cry, and the mares, looking up, beheld their new master!

*   *   *   *   *

It was well after mid-day before the stallion started to round up the mares in earnest, and after he had encircled them twice, they interpreted his wishes correctly, and moved off in a straggling column towards the ledge that spiralled the eastern cliffs to the divide.

The young stallion was now extremely careful in all he did. Once he got the foremost mares moving up the rocky trial, he did not press the remainder too firmly. He let them take their time, knowing full well that any mishap on the ledge would spell disaster, and he wanted the small herd to reach the plain on the other side of the mountain range intact.

For a leader with little experience in the handling of young mares and their colts, he showed a definite concern and care for their well being. He followed in the rear somewhat slowly, so as to give the column ample room to climb the precarious trail and pass, without panic, over the divide and into the cleft.

Only once did he experience alarm, and that was when an eagle came dropping down from the peaks above, the bird's shadow seeming more ominous than the creature itself. A half dozen or so of the mares neighed with sudden fear, and the stallion gave a sharp whistling cry as if to allay their alarm.

The moment of fear, however, was short-lived. The eagle continued to drop towards the floor of the canyon, and the mares pressing on, moved a little more quickly now as those in the lead topped the divide and passed without hesitation into the cleft.

More than a couple of hours passed before the Pahute stallion was able to pause at the divide and gaze back at the volcanic fastness far below. The afternoon was by now well spent, and heavy shadows lay in the strange labyrinth of waterholes and giant fissures. Nothing moved on the pasture where, not so long since, a band of mares had been grazing. The whole length and breadth of that fantastic glen between the two flanks of mountain was deserted, and, what was more curious, almost without substance . . . a place of oblique shadows and dark-eyed pools . . . of broken rocks and black, satanic slabs. . . .

Not long afterwards, there was no sign of life either on the eastern divide. The Pahute stallion had entered the cleft, driving the band of mares down the long corridor of the mountain towards the plain that stretched from the Quinn River Crossing in the south to the isolated uplands of the Oregon border country.

The legend of the great ghost stallion was about to be born!

CHAPTER ELEVEN

THE Pahute stallion had chosen for his new ranging territory the mountainous region of the border highlands.

It was typical wild horse country, possessing many canyons, all, for the most part running from north-west to south, and enclosed in a loop formed by Trout Creek River which had its beginnings way up in the Steens Mountains. Behind the canyons rose the massive range of the Pueblo Mountains—a continuation, in Oregon, of the Pine Forest Mountains in Nevada.

It was the distinct similarity of the two massifs that made the stallion aware of safety and gave him a sense of being on familiar ground. In addition, he felt that no better grazing could be found for a hundred miles or more.

Like his sire, Blue Streak, the Pahute stallion possessed a well-developed natural instinct for good horse country.

For the first few weeks, following the arrival of the mares in the canyon border territories, the stallion showed no further interest in them. He let them graze and wander at will, only taking them to task should they go too far from the river basin. The main refuge for the small herd was a ravine running north to south. It was roughly half a mile wide, between high mountain ridges that converged in the north, and was a full three miles in length. There was a sizeable waterhole about mid-way along the ravine, and since the grazing was rich, there was little need for the mares to wander far from the spot save on those rare occasions when they needed the greater refreshment of the river itself with its cool, swiftly running water.

The stallion, however, soon began to make short visits into adjoining canyons, all the time seeking for pasture, and also determining to his own satisfaction the safety of the locality he had chosen for the herd.

No sign of human life did he discover in his wanderings, but he did find an old trail—one of the original wagon trails striking away from the eastern skyline of mountains and making an almost straight course westward to the one great pass between the Steens Mountains and the Pueblo range.

It was not long after he had discovered the trail that he began to travel greater distances from the canyon in which the herd grazed peaceably, and always were the journeys westward in the direction of the great pass between the two main mountain escarpments.

Even as the awesome outcrop of Wild Horse Bench had attracted him back in Nevada, so now did the trail fascinate him. Day after day he traversed it, his feet treading unerringly over the very ground that hundreds of horses had trodden in those far-off days when, at the shouted commands of wagon masters, and the sharp crack of a whip, they had heaved and pulled towards the pass and the Lone Butte country that sign-pointed the route to the fabled Warner Valley and the old Oregon Trail into California.

It was while on one of his many journeys over the old wagon trail that the Pahute stallion came upon another small band of mares.

The herd saw him approaching, and took fright. The dust that rose from the mares' pounding hooves spurred the stallion into action.

To round them up was no easy task. At some period of their lives, the mares had been part of a band taken from the wild and corralled by a wrangler from a cattle ranch way up north. Indeed, they would long ago have been broken to the saddle, or sent off east but for the fact that a roan stallion had found them, and kicking the corral down, set them free.

The brutality of the roan in trying to subdue them had not been forgotten, and when he had gone off on the rampage and failed to return, the mares were not long in wandering south until they struck the rich grassland north of Trout Creek River and within close proximity to the ancient wagon trail.

Remembrances of the roan were quickly roused when they beheld the Pahute stallion heading in their direction, and when they turned in a mass and headed off north, fears as to what might happen if the strange stallion overtook them, lent speed to their running.

Even so, they were no match for Pahute.

He outran the mares and young stock until they were completely exhausted. And two days later, more animals were added to the original band the stallion had secreted in the canyon close to the southern tip of the Trout Creek River.

After a week, the newly acquired mares and their colts accepted the stallion as their leader, and soon became as quiet as the others.

When Pahute had satisfied himself that the enlarged herd could be left in safety, he set off once more to further his investigations of the ancient trail. Finally there came a day when at last the great divide between the towering walls of the two mountain ranges was less than an hour's journey away.

The stallion approached at an easy trot. Never in all his wanderings had he encountered anything quite like the scene that met his eyes.

Here was a vast opening more than a couple of miles in width, striking north-west, and clearly defined amongst the accumulated rubble of centuries was the old wagon trail. No grass grew on it, no scrub or sage. It was a sandy track running without the slightest deviation through the pass.

Almost as if to acclaim the trail's identity, the remains of a wagon lay deeply embedded in the sand, and less than a dozen feet from where he stood, the half circle of a wheel cast a crooked shadow upon the ground.

Pahute proceeded cautiously through the divide. He was both curious and watchful. He had gone scarcely more than a mile when he discovered ample evidence of the existence of both grizzly bear and elk. At one point, not far from the trail, the skull of an elk, bleached grey, with the antlers like the whitened branches of a tree that had died, protruded from amongst an over-spill of rock.

Quite close, were the remains of a bear, huddled like a very old man over a boulder, and staring with socketless eyes at the distant mountain that had witnessed his attack on the elk and the grim battle that, in the end, had brought both animals to an ignominious end.

With a shrill whinny, Pahute swung away from the grotesque remains, and hastened onwards. After another mile or so, a shelving wall of mountain sloped down from the north and the floor of the divide started to rise a little.

Even so, the trail was still clearly marked, and he had no difficulty at all in following it.

Trotting more quickly now, within an hour, he had passed the shelving mountain wall. Now the fangs of the mountain spurs ranged away on either side. From the pass, they all seemed unscalable, and were seamed and broken by the years they had known. Each separate cliff went soaring up into an immense peak, while the inner ridges swept up into what appeared to be an enormous plateau, towering high above the northern canyon country.

This as far as the Pahute stallion was concerned, was journey's end.

Pacing slowly, he moved along the foot of the cliffs and before he was actually aware of the fact, was at the very mouth of the pass with the old wagon trail spilling out into the desert like something that would never be obliterated because it had carried so much that had later become the whole history of the golden west.

The trail, however, no longer intrigued him. A lofty-walled canyon reared away into the northern fastnesses of the mountains, and in the distance was the gleam of falling water.

Moreover, there was very rich grazing indeed throughout the entire length and breadth of the canyon, with a thin sprinkling of cotton trees, the foliage of which was just beginning to change into autumnal tints.

About mid-way up the gorge, there was a deep wash, and a little beyond it, indicative of an immense volcanic disturbance at some remote stage of its history, a ravine, striking away east, appeared to be split and broken into numerous small valleys that penetrated into the main upthrust of the escarpment. At the very head of the canyon, rising in complete isolation and grandeur, the widely spread plateau dominating the northern slopes of the mountains, stood in purpling shadow.

The Pahute stallion sensed instinctively that the country he was now surveying so keenly was Wild Horse country at its best.

His ringing cry of excitement was almost his expression of approval of such utter solitude. The sound was caught up and flung from cliff to cliff, affording the animal great satisfaction. Those echoes were all that he needed to tell him that he was alone in this enormous wilderness of rock and sky. . . .

Then as he turned his head, prior to entering the canyon, his gaze became centred once more, and this time with greater concentration, on the desert Badland west of the pass and the ribbon-like shape of the old Oregon Trail striking straight across it.

The past, present and future, all seemed held captive, yet vibrantly alive as the stallion, Pahute—son of Blue Streak and direct descendant of Diablo, the devil horse—stood completely without movement, gazing out across a desert in Oregon at Beatys Butte with the curious insistence of one who was part of that three-dimensional picture that had its being in the escarpment.

*   *   *   *   *

Pahute found it exceedingly difficult to leave the locality and return to the herd he had left in the canyon adjacent to

Trout Creek River. Whilst he never ventured out beyond the limits of the pass, he could not resist standing with feet firmly pressed on the old wagon trail, staring out across the desert at the butte.

As day followed day, his early morning ritual never varied. The rocky outcrop seemed to fascinate him even more than had Wild Horse Bench. Even so, he repelled the urge to set off and visit it. Somehow, he felt that if he did indeed venture out into the desert and finally reach the butte, he would never again return to the pass and take the easterly trail back to the herd.

Then one morning, Pahute looked for the butte in vain. A sandstorm was raging out in the desert, and as if accepting this as a sign, the stallion finally set tracks for Trout Creek River, having been in the locality of the divide for more than twenty days.

He paced the old trail with an easy swing, trotting as one who knew the way as surely as he knew himself, and possessing the confidence of an animal who was truly master of this great land of mountain and desert.

No longer was he just a young stallion forming his first band of mares. In the space of twenty odd days, he had grown in stature and experience.

He was truly one of the great stallions of the legendary west!

CHAPTER TWELVE

IT WAS late in the fall before the Pahute stallion felt an inexplicable desire to drive the herd along the border territory and around the foothills of Disaster Peak to the upper reaches of the Quinn River.

He was responding to something strong in his blood—a distinct probing that drove him onwards in much the same manner as, many years before, Blue Streak himself had been driven along this same border territory in search of new grazing. In both, the instinct to travel eastwards came from the obscure knowledge inherited from their ancestors. In the days of the early ranchers, they had made profitable raids from the mountain fastnesses north of the Santa Rosa range, and as a result, had become familiar with the lush pasturelands near the river borders.

The band of mares with their rapidly growing colts, were on the move the best part of a month before Pahute decided on a canyon isolated enough to protect the herd from sudden danger. It was situated in a low range of hills a little west of the Quinn River. Apart from containing good pasture, there was a considerable amount of scrub and sage nearby to afford shelter for those colts who would assuredly require such protection from the drive of the wind from the north-east now that the shortening autumn days were quickly giving way to the harsh clutch of winter.

Already Pahute could hear the distant howls of prairie wolves way up in the hills, and sensed that soon they would be on the prowl. The mares clustered together as if for protection, and the yearlings showed distinct signs of fear.

Gazing around his new domain, the stallion realized that he had chosen well in adopting this particular range of hills for his winter sojourn. The hills whilst being broken up, were not so extensive that he could not adequately patrol them if necessary, nor were they sufficiently scattered to enable packs of wolves to gather unseen.

Pahute had indeed learnt much since acquiring the responsibility of a herd.

*   *   *   *   *

The stallion was facing the tortured uprising of the nearest hills when he smelt the first of the snow. His nostrils flared as he tested the northerly air stream. Then he swung about, and returning to the herd, started an almost ceaseless patrol for the rest of the day.

Towards evening, he made a quick decision, and rounding up both mares and yearlings, drove them to a curve in the hills that was pure cliff, rising to some five hundred feet, without any discernible break in which a mountain lion or coyote could lie hidden. There was also, within the loop, plenty of rough Buffalo grass, and below the cliffs, a run of water which Pahute sensed, would be unlikely to freeze due to the downhill slope of the watercourse and the protection it had from the rock walls abounding it in the north.

Satisfied as to the safety of the band, should heavy snow come, he circled the outer area. In this he was acting as all stallions often did when winter with its attendant dangers was not far off. It would not do to get the band snow-bound, and thus vulnerable to attack from those on the meat trail.

Scarcely four days had gone by since he had driven the herd to the Buffalo grass under the cliff when the first of the great winds from the north came driving over the hills. Within an hour of its rising, the snow came.

Even as he took in the scene with one sweeping glance, the stallion was aware that as before, he was wise in his choice of a refuge from the wind and snow. This awareness at having done well for the herd was more than apparent next morning, for although the first fall of snow lasted the whole of one night with the surrounding areas well covered, the Buffalo grass within the curve of the hill was still visible, and the mares grazing without discomfort.

There then came a short respite. The wind ceased to have a bite in it, and the snow fluttered away. Pahute, selecting a nearby hilltop as a look-out post, took up position. Now, not only could he keep the herd under close surveillance, but he could also gaze out over the white wilderness that lay between the low range of hills and the Quinn River.

Another dawn, however, found the wind once again driving in from the north. The temperature was dropping rapidly. The mares and colts turned broadside to the eddying currents that swept the natural corral, and then moved closer together for warmth.

That morning they did not see the sun. Instead, there was only a dim gathering of light in the east that disclosed great banks of cloud moving steadily before the wind. There was no colour anywhere, no shading on the mountains, no touch of green where a small copse of larch grew beside a stream. Everything was shapeless and withdrawn, and the world itself, little better than garbed in a drab twilight that was the only day it would know.

About midway through the morning, the snow came moving in with the wind, small flakes, at first, then becoming larger and hardened into spearheads of ice. The sky seemed to lower, and the snow became a bewildering pattern that enclosed the mares and their colts and shut them off from the outer limits of their refuge.

The wind continued to rise and the snow to fall. The mares pawed for the grass and were rewarded. Despite the severity of the blizzard, they were safe within the curve of the hills, and the snow was not so thickly massed as elsewhere.

Pahute alone was not within that protecting loop. He was

back on his wind-swept hill, keeping constant guard. His ears went repeatedly backwards and forwards. Afar off, rising above the wind, could be faintly heard the hunting call of some coyotes, followed by the deeper, more savage note of the prairie wolves.

They were, however, much too far off to menace the band. Moreover, judging from the fading cries, they were bent on hunting in a northerly direction.

Nevertheless, the stallion did not leave his look-out post until the day was nigh spent, and then only for an hour or so to ensure that the band was still safe and not in any discomfort.

Dawn next day was a little brighter, and Pahute on the hill was able to see far into the east. There was a glimmering brightness as if the sun would show itself. The clouds, however, were still much too dense, but one thing that glimmering on the eastern skyline revealed—the peaks of the Santa Rosa Mountains with a plume of snow streaming away from the most northerly peaks.

At the very moment the keen eyes of the stallion marked that trailing scarf in the sky, so did Jim Blaine and his father standing at their ranch door comment on it.

'I've a feeling it's going to be a stiff winter, son,' the elder man remarked.

'Seems very like it,' Jim replied, turning his gaze to the newly erected corral where four line-bred mares, recently brought in from the east, and till that morning, kept in the ranch stable, were grazing on tufts of hay.

'Look fine, don't they?' Jeff Blaine remarked with obvious satisfaction.

His son nodded thoughtfully before saying that they would not be having much of a life until the winter was over.

'Oh, I don't know,' his father answered. 'They'll manage all right. We'll give them easy exercise when we can, and on days like this, we'll keep them in the corral fer as long as we can. They sure are fine mares!'

His eyes shone with approval.

The four animals were indeed beautifully proportioned, each showing every sign of good breeding. They moved like the thoroughbreds they were as they tugged at the hay, conscious that they were being watched with admiration. Once, all four looked up, stared at the two men, and then resumed their meal.

Meanwhile, over on the northern peaks of the Santa Rosa Mountains, the plume of snow continued to flutter like a banner before suddenly streaming away on a snow-laden current of air. . . .

Book Three
The Phantom Raider

IT WAS a bad winter—not long as winters go—but very severe while the wind lay in the north. The snow continued and the passes in the hills became choked with drifts so that the marauding bands of wolves kept mainly to the northern ranges.

Whilst the wind remained steadfast, driving down from off the mountains due north, no change could be expected. It had ever been thus in the border territory—the snow persisting long after it had ceased elsewhere, and all because of the bitter sweep of the northern wind. Only when the wind swung from north to north-west, and then to west, would the snow cease and the first touch of spring come over Steens Mountains and melt the drifts surrounding Trout Creek River.

Pahute's herd remained close to the Buffalo grass grazing, not only because it was the only food remaining, but also because the wall of the mountain protected the mares who had come to hate intensely the unceasing drive of the north wind.

The winter, none the less, might indeed have passed without mishap but for the fact that some fifteen or so yearlings wandered off, and breaking into one of the snow-covered passes, managed to force an opening in one of the major drifts, thus making a clear passage from south to north.

About the same time, a band of grey timber wolves, led by a grizzled old-timer who had seen many a winter campaign far away in the north, had gathered for the hunt, all, without exception, being lean and exceedingly hungry.

The leader scented the yearlings, and stood with tail half-plumed, staring south, his nostrils searching every eddying current of air.

Because the wind was still in the north, and the young horses in the south, the scent was not so strong as it would otherwise have been; and it was only in the sudden eddies that the scent came at all to the old wolf.

The pack stood still, watching him. They too could scent the horses, but were unable to determine exactly where they were. The leader, however, was anxious to find out.

There was a glacier-like gash in the mountain close to where the pack was assembled, and the wolf made for it slowly, climbing the steep ice wall with more than calculated care. He was remembering back to a time when, in the far north, he had witnessed an over-anxious wolf slip into an ice-crevasse and lie trapped until the ice closed over him.

Malsun, as the wolf was known in the north where he had long reigned as leader of the largest pack to hunt the area, was not going to meet with a similar fate. Not only did he remember his less fortunate brethren who had died, but he remembered so much else besides, and the lesson he had learnt was that caution kept one away from danger.

Thus he trod slowly and carefully, and reached the summit of the ice acclivity without disaster.

Once there, he had no difficulty in ascertaining the whereabouts of the small band of yearling horses. The wind, funnelled through the acclivity, veered back where a cliff broke the force of its direction.

For quite fifteen minutes, Malsun stood unmoving, testing every current of air. Once he glanced back over his shoulder to make sure that the pack was not becoming restless.

Malsun whined softly in his throat. The ever veering wind currents were telling him more clearly than ever exactly where he might expect to find the horse herd. More than that, he now had a fair idea as to how far away the band was.

He whined once more, and then turning quietly and without haste, made his way back to the waiting pack.

The silent, and practically mysterious code of intelligence

that prevailed amongst their kind, told the pack what Malsun had discovered on the ice acclivity. The way the old wolf stood, with ears aslant, his head set due south and his nostrils widely flared, gave them the only clues they required to indicate the direction they should take for the meat trail.

Still they waited. One or two sat back on their haunches while the old grey wolf remained motionless, his nose still widely flared and his ears close pressed against his skull.

Then sinking back and raising his head, the leader gave the rallying call to the hunt.

Beginning low and mournful, Malsun's call went resounding across the wastes of snow and mountain. All living things within a ten mile radius heard that call of the grey wolves to the meat trail.

Again and again was it repeated, a call that seemed to increase in volume until the world of the wild acknowledged its importance, and shivered.

Whilst those that feared, shrank into every likely hole for protection, those of the wolf brethren for whom it was intended, rejoiced. In a little while, wolf calls were sounding from both north and west, and the grey legion of the wild began to gather for the hunt.

Meanwhile, Malsun and his own pack, sat and waited. This was the law of the grey wolves—that, in times of famine, he who had discovered meat, should rally all distant blood brothers and lead them to the feast. Apart from that, experience had taught Malsun that a large pack would be better able to bring down a herd of wild horses such as he had scented.

They were like grey shadows in a white wilderness that was without colour or tangible shape.

A sudden scurry of wind, whipped up the snow, flinging fine glistening particles all about the waiting pack. The wolves blinked, but not one shifted his position.

Then at last, the first of the beasts that heard Malsun's call came slinking in, soon to be followed by others . . . grey, silent creatures who in a short while would be running without a sound at the heels of their leader.

The winter's day was more than half spent when the pack finally set off. No living thing witnessed its unhurried departure. One moment the wolves were sitting in a semi-circle, then they were up and away, with Malsun setting the pace, running with tail full plumed. . . .

*   *   *   *   *

The call of the grey hunters had, however, been heard by one for whom it was not intended.

Pahute, on his look-out post, heard it searching down from the high hills of the north. In the moment that he turned his head the better to hear, so did he manage to catch the far-off answering calls. They seemed to come from the most remote places, but because the cold upper atmosphere acted as a sounding-board, the stallion could hear them quite distinctly. The very pounding of his heart instilled into him the knowledge that there was indeed a great gathering of the grey legion of the wild.

He became filled with an increasing unrest. So many wolf calls continued to peal off those northerly hills that he decided to visit the herd and remain amongst the mares so as to be ready to ward off any danger that might threaten them.

It was not long before he discovered that some of the yearlings were missing. Numerous hoof marks indicated the route they had taken.

Pahute was not satisfied. They might have taken a wandering trail up into the foothills. With a view to finding them quickly, he ignored the hoof prints and raising his head, ascertained the approximate whereabouts of the strays.

By now, the wolf calls had ceased. Some inherent instinct warned the stallion that this, in itself, was ominous. The pack was on the move, and therefore travelling silently.

Pahute sprang into immediate action. Ignoring the frightened mares and their colts, he went into a swinging trot, and was soon up amongst the broken foothills. In no time, he came to the place where the snow had been churned up and scattered by kicking hooves. Pressing on, he found that an entrance had been forced through an immense drift to one of the main divides. Not many minutes later, Pahute came upon the yearlings.

Sorely alarmed, they stood crouched against an ice wall, with heads set in the direction of the north. They too had heard the wolf calls of an hour since, and now, fearful, sought protection by massing close together.

Pahute shrilled out a cry of anger. One glance at the cliff above the strays told him that they were in the most vulnerable spot for an attack.

The wall, thick with snow and ice, sloped away towards the head of the pass. It required but one of the wolves to strike it as he came up over the divide, and the rest would follow as a matter of course. Inside of a minute, the entire pack would be in a position to go into the attack, pouring down upon the strays from a break in the cliff which was not more than three feet above them.

Pahute plunged, continuing to scream his disapproval and anger. His forefeet struck up at the uprising wall of ice before he turned his whole attention to the young horses.

It was at this moment that Malsun, running swiftly and silently, came up over the lip of the pass. Behind him, spread out like a huge fan, some twenty odd wolves were loping in easy strides.

The entire pack halted when Malsun came to an abrupt stop. Ears that had been carried erect until then, lay suddenly aslant in apprehension, and tails sank slowly until they hung sabre-like behind hind legs splayed out for a good stance and balance on the hard-stacked snow.

Red-eyed, and ravenously hungry, the pack stared over the

edge of the pass, glimpsing not only the young horses, but the stallion also. It was then that they sensed that it was going to be no easy kill after all.

The exertion the wolves had expended in coming from all points of the compass at Malsun's bidding, seemed of little significance against the physical wrack of hunger they experienced. The slow process of starvation had long since passed the stage of torment. They had become used to it, and only an inner weakness reminded them that they had not eaten for some time. Thus, now that they had stopped running, more than one felt the inexplicable urge to lie down in the snow. Their lean sides heaved with their heavy breathing, and their tongues protruding through widely gaping jaws darted to and fro as if each and every one was already tasting the warm flesh of the horses.

But for the strange weariness within them, and Malsun's curious attitude of vigilance, some would indeed have gone racing in amongst the herd and rent each member limb from limb.

Malsun was fully aware of the pack's uncertainty. Even so, he did not make an unexpected move. He was slowly sizing up the situation. He did not like the look of the stallion who now stood directly between the wolves and the horses. Whilst in other circumstances, a surprise attack might have had a decisive effect, it could be otherwise when a maddened stallion went into the offensive. More than that, Malsun knew that the pack was hunger-weary, and might be quite unable to bring down the young horses in face of the opposition from the stallion.

The old wolf was very wise indeed. He had made many attacks on wild horses in the past, and remembered the defeats as he remembered so many other things.

Then the very thing he feared, happened. The stallion had turned without warning, and racing swiftly into the very centre of the strays, got them milling around in a serried mass.

This was more than the wolves behind Malsun could stand. They surged past their leader to make a sharp and relentless attack. . . .

Nothing quite like it had ever been attempted before by a pack of wolves who, ignoring the leader, had gone into an attack without any resemblance of strategy governing either action or method of assault.

Malsun, with the pack streaming past him, turned his head to snap at those who crowded too closely against him. His jaws bit empty air. The wolves were much too intent on making a kill to retaliate, and avoided him.

Then, with the entire pack, save its leader, streaming down into the narrow limits of the pass, Pahute's reactions were instantaneous. He did, what on another, but completely different occasion, his sire had done. He swung about, rearing and plunging. He then drove the yearlings before him . . . a racing, shrieking band that thrust straight into the midst of the wolves.

So great had been the initial impetus of the pack that it was unprepared for the sudden surging forward of the horses. Before it could check its pace, or turn to escape the threshing hooves, the young horses, with Pahute now amongst them, were rearing and plunging above it, beating the wolves underfoot.

By now, the whole of the pass was a seething press of bodies. The snow was no longer white, but red. The wolves, leaderless, were at the mercy of the fear-maddened horses. As Pahute drove the herd around and around, the wolves, enclosed in the ever narrowing circle, essayed various means of escape only to find that the gap they had momentarily glimpsed was as suddenly closed, and that a plunging horse was towering over them.

One screaming horse went down, a wolf at its throat, but before the beast could get a firm grip on the jugular, he was shaken off. As the fallen horse struggled to rise, Pahute had trampled his attacker under his pounding hooves.

In all this time, Malsun remained on the lip of the pass. Then unexpectedly, he went racing down into the arena. Almost too late his effort to save the remnant of the pack. Already more than half the wolves were lying in a mangled mass beneath the ceaseless surge of feet, with another eight or nine severely injured, and dragging broken limbs.

Just when it seemed that nothing could save the remaining wolves from disaster, Pahute turned about, and in a matter of seconds, he had the yearlings flying down the pass, the stallion himself hard at their heels.

Of their number, three had been slain by the wolves. Some two or three others had gashes in their flanks. For the rest, they had escaped without visible injury. One lesson, however, had been learnt. But for Pahute they would have met a terrible death. This knowledge went with them as they continued to race away from the scene of the attack, and was clearly expressed in the rolling of their eyes, and the cloud of vapour that rose from their over-heated bodies. . . .

CHAPTER FOURTEEN

NOTHING further threatened Pahute's herd for the rest of the winter which, in less than a month, was fast giving way to brighter skies and a constantly veering wind which now blew mainly from the west. As soon as the snow began to soften up a little, and the area from Trout Creek River down to the Quinn showed more green than white, the stallion bestirred himself and went ranging for new pastures.

Since the Quinn River lay in the watershed of a low sweep of hill country penetrating down to Rebel Creek, Pahute decided to drive the band due south, sensing that between the mountains and the river, the grassland would be abundant with the coming of the warmer weather.

Spring was well established along the western hills when Pahute finally brought his herd down across the borderlands of Oregon and Nevada. Due to the rapid melting of the snows, the Quinn was flowing swiftly with a heavy surge of water, and the stallion knew that even had he so desired, he would have been unable to drive the band across to the eastern bank.

Thus he kept the herd on the western shore, and followed the low range of hills which, day by day, was changing shape and colour as the last of the snow went, and the grey of the rocks changed to a verdant green where dwarf cedar straddled the broken divides.

The change from winter to spring was startling in effect. The skies were blue once more, and at mid-day, the sun was hot. Long before Pahute and his herd reached Rebel Creek, the old harsh colour sequence of both desert and mountain was once again the feature of the Nevada uplands, and the

stallion was possessed of a vague feeling of familiarity about
the route he followed.

It was so like the many other trails he had known before in
Nevada, with the hill country becoming more and more broken
as it approached the desert land that lay between Rebel Creek
and Quinn River Crossing.

As if to give the stallion an even greater sense of familiarity, the last of the hill groups ended in another spiral
upthrust of rocks, similar in pattern to Wild Horse Bench,
although perhaps, not quite so high, nor quite so extensive.
Nevertheless, the outcrop was certainly similar in appearance to that other bench he had known, and for him, just as
intriguing.

By now, Pahute's band comprised of some thirty mares,
and a like number of colts, while yearlings totalled another
sixteen.

Altogether, it was quite a large herd that seemed to have
grown without the stallion being actually aware of it taking
place. As a result, it was most important that exceptionally
good grazing was soon available, and this Pahute found where
the hill country ended, and the desert began.

It was a rich stretch of grassland, running right from the
western bank of the Quinn into a vast canyon-like basin that
lay inside the encircling loops of the mountain country west
of the range he and the band had been following. Moreover,
by proceeding some little way up the basin, the stallion was
at the western pinnacles of the bench that had reminded him
so forcibly of Wild Horse Bench.

Pahute sensed that there could be little better country for
many miles around; and thus the band found refuge in a
place where, so often before in the past, other herds of wild
horses had sought similar refuge when the year was young and
the Quinn River ran swiftly with flood water. Thus too, was
the stallion close to another bench with its mystery and lure,
and from the bench, on its eastern side, running direct to a

ford across the river, was a trail that led to the distant Santa
Rosa Mountains and Jeff Blaine's cattle ranch. . . .

*   *   *   *   *

The spring was nigh done and summer moving slowly over
the hills of the west when Pahute experienced the old urge to
go on the rampage. He had grown increasingly restless as the
days lengthened and the call of all wild things became more
and more insistent as kind sought kind, and the birds of the
air started to teach their young to fly.

Times there were when the stallion, to allay the acute
restlessness that was upon him, raced out into the desert,
tearing through little thickets of dwarf cedar, leaping over
small gullies and splashing through streams that were still
turbulent as they flowed down to the Quinn. Then suddenly,
these brief excursions satisfied him no longer. The band was
in excellent shape, and, for the time being at least, well able
to be left unattended.

With this knowledge strong in him, he sought to give
expression to his restlessness by becoming completely free
of the herd for a while. Accordingly, one morning, before
sun-up, Pahute set out and hit the trail for the Santa Rosa
Mountains.

No divided memory had he of the mares and their colts as
he trotted eagerly eastward, no idea of seeking out further
mares, and certainly no idea of raiding the homesteads of
man. He went at a firm, but unhurried pace, running for
the sheer joy of being on the move, his white tail streaming
out behind him, his mane floating over his shoulder like a
cloud.

Anyone seeing him from a distance would have declared
him to be 'no real hoss' at all, but one from the far-off ranges
of the sky. Indeed, before a week was out, such would be the
description given of him to cattlemen in the Santa Rosa

Mountain area. . . . Not yet 'Ghost Hoss', but 'wild hoss from the sky ranges. . . .'

Pahute was in grand fettle as he continued eastward. He crossed the Quinn River at a point a little below the natural fording spot, swimming with ease and striking out for the opposite shore with the unerring instinct of one who knew that as long as he travelled eastward towards the mountains he would never be far from good grazing and fresh water. . . .

Pahute struck the first of the unfenced range country of the Blaine ranch late one afternoon. The sun was well down the sky, and although no shadows were apparent, there was just that quietness resting over everything that was the peace of early evening.

There were no cattle visible, and no indication of life to warn the stallion that for the first time he was approaching the territories of man. Directly ahead, rising up magnificently in tiers and enormous cliffs, was the main escarpment of the Santa Rosa Mountains. Parts of the nearby slopes appeared to be covered with pine and alder, and from the range territory at which the stallion viewed them, were clearly broken up into deeply recessed canyons.

The horse liked this new country. He stood for seconds testing the wind, and then, instinctively, moved a little south-east until he came to a fresh-water pond of some extent.

By now the sun had gone; the quick twilight that came from the east soon deepened into night: and with a million, million stars gleaming brightly above him, Pahute rolled over on to his side and slept, while a nightbird called from beside the pool, and a new moon came up over the highest peak on the Santa Rosa Mountains.

The stallion spent a very quiet night on the Blaine range territory. When morning came, however, he stood knee-deep in a silver mist that had risen from the pool during the night, and looked every bit the 'hoss that had come down from the far-off ranges of the sky'. . . .

* * * * *

The Blaine ranch was set on level ground close to a small creek. The building was low-built and rambling, but for all that, very roomy, with a long veranda that looked out over a wide valley which, at most times of the year, was filled with cattle.

Back of the ranch, the foothills leading to the high sweep of the Santa Rosa Mountains, rose within half a mile of the barns and corrals, and to shelter the ranch from the sudden squalls that often swept down the many abutting canyons, a wood of larch and alder had been planted to some effect. Not only did it serve the purpose of keeping the ranch house warm in winter, but in spring and fall, it gave a startling beauty to the stark uprising of rock and cliff. The vivid green of the larches was in startling contrast to the seamed red and lichen-grey slopes that rolled both north and south.

Indeed, the ranch was, as Jeff Blaine often declared, built just where a man would wish to spin out the rest of his days.

Young Jim was inclined to agree with him, no woman yet having crossed his path to make him think otherwise.

Pahute came up on the ranch house from a point a little north-west, striking the wood which gave him ample protection. He could hear, away off, the sullen murmur of the river as it rolled through the creek, and what seemed more important, somewhere, a mile, maybe two away, the bawling of cattle.

He could not quite identify these distant calls, having no intimate experience of cattle generally. None the less, he was interested. The sounds spoke of life which he certainly did understand, and as a result, he started to walk warily through the wood, pushing his way resolutely under the overhanging branches of the alders, scratching himself in places, but not feeling any hurt because of his rising excitement.

At last he came to the edge of the wood and gazed down, startled, upon the low barn buildings and the ranch house itself.

In all his wanderings, he had never seen anything like them before, and the rising spiral of smoke from the bunk house chimney, caused him momentarily, to move back a pace or two, his ears twitching nervously, his nostrils widely flared.

He caught the scent of wood smoke, and once again was aware of a queer sense of alarm. Somewhere, he felt he had known such a smell before, but he could not determine where or when. Once more, however, it was not he who was remembering, but a singing in his bloodstream that reminded him, bringing alive the memories those who had been his forebears had known, and feared.

Indeed, the fear Blue Streak had of man was in the nervous beating of his heart . . . the fear too that Diablo had once known for his Apache master. . . .

Then quite suddenly, all nervousness departed from Pahute. His eyes became centred on one of the corrals, and he saw the four line-bred mares which had become the pride of the Blaine ranch. They were grazing peaceably, no veering wind-currents bringing to them the stain of the stallion from the wild who was so close by.

Pahute shook himself, his ears no longer twitching. He turned about in the darkness under the trees, and then faced once more the open land, with the wide sweep of the valley beyond the ranch buildings, and the corral—much nearer—containing the four mares.

He moved forward slowly, a fine, upstanding shape of a horse, his white stockinged legs rising and falling, lifting the hooves and dropping them again without a sound upon the pine-needle floor.

Farther and farther away from the copse did he go in his slow, measured pacing, his sides rising with anxiety lest he startle the mares, his eyes bright and never once losing sight of them. Pahute could hear no more the sounds of the cattle bawling. The ranch lands, and the wide valley beyond, lay serene and bright in sunlight; only over the distant mountain peaks was a rain cloud breaking, and sending, as the shadows dropped, a mist of rain and hail on the lower foothills.

Then the mares saw the stallion for by now, he was quite close to the corral. They paused in their grazing, and viewed him with wonder. He was so utterly different from any of the ranch horses. They sensed immediately his lawless nature, but could not refrain from moving up to the very edge of the corral the better to see him.

Perhaps for thirty seconds the mares stared through the palisade. Maybe it was longer. Time seemed no longer of importance. In that minute, or less, the rain and hail came sweeping over the intervening land, bringing greyness where before there had been bright sunlight. A brisk wind was driving the deluge forward; the smoke from the bunk house chimney wavered and went flying out in blue whorls across the valley.

The stallion felt the sting of the hail on his body as he made a savage rush forward, and a moment later, he was kicking at the palisade to get at the mares. His great feet pounded the stakes, and as he turned, the better to kick out with his hind legs, he was fortunate in finding a weak spot in one of the main supports. In less than a couple of minutes, the palisade was being trampled down, while the now badly frightened mares whinnied and screamed with terror.

There were sounds of voices from the bunk house; somebody called for a gun.

Even as Jeff Blaine and his son came racing from the

ranch house, and Jake, the cowman, from the bunk house, ~~Pahute had broken~~ into the corral and was rounding up the mares.

He moved swiftly and with vicious intent. He required the mares to obey him instantly, and they quickly interpreted the meaning of his short runs around them. Accustomed as they were to the more leisurely, and certainly less savage movements of the ranch stock, they were driven by fear to move in the direction indicated by Pahute who was plunging and bringing his immense hooves within an inch or two of their flanks. When it seemed the stallion must maim or kill them with his savage lunges, they moved away together—the four mares and the stallion from the wild. The very moment they were free of the broken palisade, Pahute sent them racing towards the distant copse and into the thickening haze of rain and hail. . . .

Jeff Blaine and Jim, with Jake stumbling behind them, were too far away to take any decisive action. All they could see was a jumble of shapes, pursued by a stallion who, as he disappeared into the haze, was little more than a phantom, with a white tail streaming out behind him, and the toss of a white mane over a neck that was thrust out in an ominous manner towards the fleeing mares. . . .

Jake cried out, almost on bated breath: 'A wild hoss from the ranges of the sky. . . .'

Jim shouted: 'Sure! He's plumb wild. . . .'

The elder Blaine, bemoaning his mares, muttered with suppressed anger: 'Wild hoss from the sky, did you say? Not he . . . he's real enough. . . .'

All three men had come to a stumbling halt, panting heavily.

'He could be the Pahute hoss,' Jake began. 'I've heard tell of a stallion the like of that one, come from Pahute Peak way over agin High Rock Lake. . . . A son of Blue Streak. . . .'

Jeff Blaine turned on his heels, obstinate, angry. 'Go saddle up, Jim,' he ordered his son. 'You'll be hitting the trail after wild hosses sure enough this trip . . . and at the end of it, there'll be one wild hoss the less, believe me. . . .'

Half an hour later, the great pursuit was on.

CHAPTER FIFTEEN

WITH half a dozen ranch hands in addition to his son, Jim, and the cowman, Jake, Jeff Blaine was on the trail in less than an hour from the stallion's departure from the corral.

By now, he was less inclined to be spurred on by anger, accepting the fact that if he were to get back his mares, he would have to proceed not only with caution, but with a cunning likely to match the stallion's own. He knew too that it might not be an easy journey he was making, and to safeguard himself against any unexpected mishap, he took with him two extra horses, using them as pack animals.

No matter how long it took, he was fully determined to get back those mares of his.

The small band of men, with Jeff and Jake in the lead, came out of the copse at a point half a mile above that taken by Pahute. There was no sign of the stallion, or the mares, in the first stretch of unfenced country that met their eyes, and Jeff was forced to cast around for some trace of hoof marks likely to set them on the right trail.

It was Jake, however, with his uncanny instinct for reading signs on the ground, that came to the very spot when the horse and the mares had broken cover. Some moist droppings made him doubly sure, and he summoned the others.

Jeff Blaine was satisfied. He knew Jake was a good man. In the past, there had been times when he trailed missing cattle for many days, finally coming up on them in some secluded spot where many another man would never have dreamt of looking.

He had not the slightest doubt but what Jake would find the mares, and that they would be back in another corral before sun-down. But Blaine had not reckoned on the sagacity of Pahute.

A couple of hours or so after high noon, Jake signalled the men to halt. 'I'll make a survey of the land from the top of that ridge,' he said, indicating a low reef of rock cutting away from the trail in a northerly direction.

Without further parley, he drove his horse forward quietly, halting only when within a few yards of the ridge. Jake then dismounted, and putting his horse to graze on a patch of Buffalo grass, proceeded to clamber up the rock formation on hands and knees.

Just before he reached the summit, he paused and glanced back. His companions were watching him, not more than a quarter of a mile away.

Jake then pushed his way up to the very edge of the formation.

He gasped, and crouched back below the ridge. Pahute and the mares were drinking from the fresh-water pond the stallion had discovered the previous night.

The wind was coming in from the west, and the stallion received no warning that he was being spied upon. He was drinking from the pool as if he had all the time in the world at his disposal.

Jake was mystified. He had never before heard of an all wild horse showing so little concern after such an audacious raid on a ranch. He could only surmise that Pahute, till that day, had experienced no direct encounter with man, and therefore had no knowledge of what man could do to him. Mebbe, he would be easy to round up on that account. Mebbe not! You could never tell with wild horses. Ole Colorado Ted had said over and over again that any wild hoss . . . or mustang, would rather die than give up his freedom and submit to the rope and halter. Mebbe that was just what would happen if anybody made a throw with a rope at the stallion down there by the pond.

Jake remained hidden behind the ridge, watching every move the horse made. He found himself taking in every line of the stallion's appearance, admiring his straight back and high-placed head. There was a tantalizing thought going through his brain that this stallion would never wear a saddle. Moreover, Jake could tell, even at a very casual glance, that the hoss was no ordinary mustang. He had breeding in every line of him . . . pride too, born of a long line of aristocratic ancestors. . . . There was also that blue-black colour that again was no ordinary colour . . . just like Blue Streak. . . . Jake stiffened at the thought.

There came to him quite forcibly the fact that he had not been mistaken when he told old man Blaine that mebbe it was a son of Blue Streak that had taken his mares. The hoss he was now looking at could be none other than a son of that old-time stallion that had menaced the ranching country for some years now.

He did not know whether to feel apprehensive about the discovery, or glad. One thing was certain! The hoss down there by the pond could be just as great a menace as his sire, perhaps more so because of his youth.

This new range stallion was a strange sort of animal. It was odd that he should possess such a white mane and tail when the rest of him was blue-black. Then there were the white stockings to the animal's legs! Another distinctive characteristic reminiscent of Blue Streak. . . .

Jake scratched his chin once more. He had to admit it. He was completely enamoured with the horse. Raider or not . . . there couldn't be another like him in the whole of Nevada . . . or for that matter, in Oregon, unless it were Blue Streak whom no man had ever subdued though many had tried.

As if he could no longer bear the sight of such a splendid horse so near yet, for him, so far, Jake began to lower himself down the rocks. When he remounted his own animal and rode back to Jeff Blaine and the others, he was in a thoughtful mood.

The rancher was, by this time, most impatient at the delay. He-thought Jake had wasted too much time on the ridge. When he heard what the cowman had to say, he was sure of it.

'Why didn't you signal us to join you?' he asked sharply. Jake shook his head decisively.

'It wouldn't hev done any good, boss,' he answered. 'We just can't rush things. We've got to move quiet-like, otherwise, if thet hoss gets moving with them mares, we'll never catch up with them.'

'What do you think we ought to do then?'

'We must ride up to the ridge quietly an' then spread out. Some of us can ride around the rocks from the south . . . the others from the north. Our best chance is to encircle the pond and cut out the stallion. We can then drive them mares back to the ridge and rope 'em. One thing is certain, boss. You'll never get a rope around the neck of that stallion. He ain't born fer breakin' in.'

'Do you suggest we should let him get away?' Blaine asked incredulously.

'It would be best, boss,' Jake answered quietly.

Blaine grunted angrily.

'Get moving!' he ordered harshly.

He swung his horse around, and signalling the others to follow, rode forward in the direction of the ridge.

* * * * *

At the foot of the ridge the men halted. Jake and Jeff Blaine dismounted together.

'I'm going to look over that ridge,' the rancher said abruptly.

'I'm comin' with you,' Jim swung himself down from the saddle. 'After all, I'm just as interested in them mares as you are, Dad.'

The elder Blaine nodded, and signified to Jake to lead the way.

'We must move quietly,' the cowman said by way of caution, and proceeded to clamber up the rocks, followed by Jeff Blaine and his son, while the others remained on their horses watching.

Not a man in that party of ranch hands could conceal his eagerness to glimpse, and maybe meet up with the wild hoss that had dared break into old man Blaine's corral and make off with four of his best mares.

The very audacity of the action was something that demanded the respect of every man who had dealings with horses, either saddle broken or wild.

Meanwhile, Jake and the Blaines had reached the summit of the ridge and were anxiously peering over. The Pahute stallion was still at the pool, and the four mares were attempting to graze within a dozen yards of him. That they were nervous was obvious from the glances they continually gave him.

The mares had been driven hard. Jeff Blaine could see that by the way they breathed. Their sides heaved with every step they took. Even so, they were far from blown. At a move from the stallion, they would be off at a fine pace, and, as Jake had remarked, would be difficult to overtake.

Jeff Blaine let his gaze concentrate on the stallion.

'I've never seen a hoss lookin' so grand before,' he said at last and gently, speaking more to himself than the others. 'He's sure got class. . . .'

'He's a sure son o' Blue Streak,' Jake took the opportunity of saying once again.

'He's all of what you said, Jake,' he remarked at last, 'a really great stallion. . . .' he broke off.

The wind must have swung completely around. Less than a minute or so before he had felt it blowing straight into his face—a stiffish breeze too that had in it the warmth of the desert. Now it was coming from behind him . . . a much cooler flow of wind that obviously was streaming from off the snow-covered peaks of the Santa Rosa Mountains.

Both Jake and Jimmie were aware of the sudden change in the direction of the wind. So too was Pahute! His head went up, and he half turned so that he stood staring across the pond at the ridge. There was suspicion in the sudden movement of the muscles in his legs. He was poised for flight. His nostrils flared, and his ears went forward a trifle. All three men could see clearly the wild light of mingled terror and anger springing up in his eyes.

He was absolutely motionless, like an animal frozen in death. Never in his life before had he appeared so magnificent.

Sudden apprehension had tightened every sinew and muscle in Pahute's body. Every single part of him was still, his stance that of an animal on the alert, yet, in his very alertness, aggressively defiant. It was as though he were telling the very wind that blew over him that he was a free being in a free world of mountain and prairie, and that he would submit to none!

Only the white mane suddenly lifted in the flow of the wind . . . lifted and fluttered a little as the breeze, like invisible fingers, rippled through it.

Then a cloud—remnant of the storm that, earlier, had brought rain and hail sweeping down on to the plains—brushed past the burnished face of the sun. A shadow—very dark indeed because of the intensity of the sunlight that had preceded it—came leaping up the ridge on a new surge of the wind. The gloom spilled over into the fresh-water pond which, instantly, became a darkened mirror, possessing neither movement nor reflection. In that same moment, the blue-black stallion became all black—the tail and mane only seeming to retain some of the sunlight that had been so abruptly taken away.

It was then that the stallion already called 'Pahute' by Jake, got the name that was to be his for as long as he lived. Indeed, it was to be a name that would continue long in the annals of wild horse history alongside that of Diablo and Blue Streak.

Dark Fury and Silver Star, being mentioned by many an old-timer when the last of the wild horse herds had been driven by man from the great prairies of the west. And, oddly enough, it was again Jake who gave it to him on that very day when the stallion stood beside a darkened pond in the unfenced grassland adjacent to the Santa Rosa Mountains.

'Ghost Hoss!' Jake said on bated breath. 'Ghost Hoss!'

The rancher and his son looked at him inquiringly.

'Not stallion from the sky ranges?' Blaine queried softly.

The cowman shook his head.

'Nope,' said he. 'Just Ghost Hoss, for that's what he is. . . .'

And Pahute had at last read the warning in the wind. Uttering a scream of defiant anger, he charged at the mares, and was driving them with all speed across the unfenced rangeland, still continuing to scream with anger and moving like the wind itself at daybreak when whipped to the fury of a gale. . . .

CHAPTER SIXTEEN

Pahute had the mares well under control and fleeing before him.

His snort of anger and shrill screams had been quite sufficient to let the mares know that he would brook no deviation from a straight run westward. Thus they were well set on the trail and running swiftly by the time Blaine and his ranch hands had rounded the ridge and set off in pursuit.

With each stride, the stallion was showing his pursuers only too clearly that any hope they had of overtaking him had far better be abandoned. In less than twenty minutes from the stampede from the pond, the stallion and mares were little more than specks in the rolling immensity of the plain that was now taking complete possession of what Blaine fondly called 'the outer unfenced lands'.

Even so, despite the gruelling pace the Pahute stallion was setting, Jeff Blaine was not prepared to give up. The habitual humour in his eyes had gone. In its place was a strange doggedness. More than that, he sat in the saddle with a deal less ease than was his usual habit. Jake, glancing at him as he raced alongside, saw that his employer was taut and nervous. Admiration for the stallion had given way to a gnawing anxiety for the safety of his mares.

Jake suddenly pulled his horse to a halt, and Blaine, wondering what was amiss, did the same. Then the entire band of ranch hands had gathered around, their horses snorting and breathing heavily.

'We can't keep this up, boss,' the cowman explained. 'We'll not only run our horses off their legs, but we'll become saddle-sore at the pace we're making.'

'Do you want that stallion to get away with my mares?' the rancher almost shouted.

'Nope, but we'll do no good tearing off after him like this. We'll only scare him worse than ever.'

'Jake's right, Dad,' Jim said.

Blaine was at a loss for words. He seemed almost shrunken as he sat loosely in the saddle. As he shaded his eyes from the brightness of the western sky, he could now no longer see the stallion or the mares. Only a cloud of dust rose out there in the west like a faint haze of smoke drifting upwards so soon to be gone.

'What now?' he asked at last.

'Take it more easy, boss,' Jake answered sympathetically. 'We'll just trail the hoss. His tracks'll not be hard to follow. Then mebbe we'll come up on him when he's off his guard. As I see it, we're bound to catch up with him by the Quinn. He sure can't cross the river without lookin' for the regular fording point. . . . Not with them mares, anyway. . . .'

'We'll leave it to you,' Blaine answered slowly, staring once again into the west. 'You're a good trail finder,' he added.

'Thanks, boss,' Jake replied.

They camped that night near the thickest scattering of greasewood that could be found along the trail blazed by Pahute and the mares. All the men were saddle-sore, and weary, and were glad to bed down as soon as they had eaten.

Jake and Jeff Blaine were silent. Neither felt disposed to discuss the matter of the stallion, nor talk about any of the problems they had encountered. Soon, like the others, they too were asleep.

Not so Jim Blaine. His mind was much too active to permit him to sleep. All he seemed able to do was remember that at last he was on the track of a 'real wild hoss'. The very mention of the name 'wild hoss' thrilled him deep down. Whenever he did close his eyes, all he could see was the stallion racing away with the mares, and ahead of the stallion, vague, but nevertheless stamped with its own particular identity—Wild Horse Bench!

Jimmie felt that one day, he would see Wild Horse Bench again, and then, mebbe, a whole herd of wild horses would be hidden in its winding corridors. . . . Not just one horse, but a whole herd . . . a whole herd. . . .

The thought passed and repassed through his mind, and as he lay on his back, staring up at the stars, he found himself recalling what Jake had said of the stallion when he first saw him. . . . 'Hoss from the sky ranges. . . .' Now it was that other, more impressive name. . . .'Ghost Hoss!'

It seemed to Jimmie, on reflection, that there was very little difference in either name. Both summed up the same horse . . . that beautiful stallion whom Jake swore was a son of the fabled Blue Streak.

He found himself caught up by the magic of the night sky so far above him. There was one place in it where no flickering of stars was visible. It was a passage of utter darkness, striking away westward.

Jimmie's tired eyes followed that track of velvet blackness. Then something moved across it . . . sweeping away westward in an arc of trailing light . . . . Like a stallion, Jim thought, racing away to the very edge of the world. . . . There were mist shadows then, passing across the stars . . . shadows like the galloping of numberless horses, lean creatures, surely, all with flying manes and swishing tails . . . horses moving across the great ranges of the sky. . . .

His lips framed one word 'Ah!'

Afar off, a coyote called. The horses tethered close to the greasewood, moved restlessly. One whinnied softly. A little wind murmured in the scrub. Then Jim Blaine heard no more the coyote's call nor the movement of the horses. The murmur of the wind was little else but the shuddering of his own breath in his throat as his eyelids dropped in heavy sleep.

He did not move until dawn.

*   *   *   *   *

The rancher and his men were up early. Jeff Blaine did not intend to let the stallion get too far on the trail.

After a hasty breakfast, the horses were again saddled, and with Jake in the lead, the pursuit was continued, the pace being set at an easy gallop the very instant the cowman picked up definite signs that they were still on the actual trail taken by Pahute and the mares.

The route was due west, and by mid-day, Jake was sure they'd pick up the stallion at Quinn River. Whilst above, the sky was cloudless, over in the north-west there was heavy cloud, and the far-off mountains were lost in the masses of drifting vapour that broke over them.

'If it rains up there in the north-west,' Jake remarked with satisfaction, 'that hoss'll find the Quinn running fast with flood water, an' mebbe he'll hev to wait a bit before attempting a crossing.'

Blaine hoped it would be so.

By nightfall, the rancher and his men were within a few miles of the Quinn. Up to now, the stallion's trail had been easy enough to follow, and Jake predicted that next day they would be sure to catch up with him. That the clouds in the north-west had indeed broken in torrential rain was evident enough during the afternoon when distant rumbles of thunder and bright lightning flashes on the horizon told of the storm raging in the mountains.

Another camp was set up for the night a little east of Rebel Creek. By now, the men having become accustomed to the exceptionally arduous riding conditions, sat around the camp-fire talking a while before turning in. The conversation was of one thing—the pursuit!

Not one of them sitting around that camp-fire had any doubts as to the ultimate outcome of the adventure. Old man Blaine was dead set on getting his mares back, and at the same time, either catching the stallion, or killing him. They all hoped that Blaine or Jake would succeed in catching the horse. Not that the cowman viewed the prospect with any enthusiasm. He said over and over again that the stallion was never intended for the halter, that he would fight the rope like fury itself, and would never submit to having a saddle put on him.

'He'll fight, an' mebbe die for his freedom,' was Jake's last comment; and the others were inclined to agree with him.

Jeff Blaine, however, had the last word.

'Best decide it one way or the other when we catch up with him,' he said, yawning.

*   *   *   *   *

Next morning Jim rolled out of his blankets before the others were awake, and sat up rubbing his eyes. After a few minutes, he strolled over to a small waterhole where he stood for a long while gazing out across the desert and scrub in the direction of the Quinn River. The flaring of the dawn in the east was being reflected upon the mountain spurs in the west. He guessed that in one or other of the canyons of that distant mountain range the stallion they were pursuing had his herd hidden away.

'We'll catch up with him today, son,' said a voice beside him, and he started so lost was he in his thoughts.

'Seems likely we shall,' he agreed, after a pause. Then, seeking to clarify his own position as regards the stallion, he added: 'Once we've got hold of them mares, we can be heading it back home. We needn't concern ourselves with the stallion.'

'No?'

There was a note of inquiry in the elder Blaine's voice.

'No!' Jim answered at once. 'We don't want him at all, Dad, and anyway, from what Jake says, he would be no good as a saddle hoss. He'd more'n likely break us before we break him.'

'Well, we'll see. Now best get moving, son. Breakfast is cooking and it smells mighty good to me.'

*   *   *   *   *

Not long afterwards, the rancher and his party were once again on the trail. All were now convinced that before noon, they would meet up with the stallion and the mares.

Jeff Blaine had been riding without any conscious effort, sitting slack in the saddle. Whilst he had been thrashing out in his mind the problem of the stallion's possible grazing territory, the band of riders had been steadily approaching the river basin.

Suddenly there was a shout from Jim!

'Look!'

Blaine pulled his horse to a halt with a jerk. Ahead, was the wide loop of the river. The foreground was mesquite-covered desert beyond which was clearly more fertile soil . . . and grassland. . . .

Blaine's face lit up and elation glowed in his eyes. His knuckles gleamed white under the skin as he gripped the reins tightly and began perceptibly to pull at his horse's bridle.

Standing by the river, beyond the mesquite, and staring directly at him and his men, was the stallion, and bunched behind him, the four mares.

Even from where he was, Blaine could see that the river was running in heavy spate and that the stallion was disconcerted because of it. Both Jim and Jake were conscious of the same fact. The ranch hands too thought that the swiftly flowing river would bring about the stallion's downfall, for he dare not cross it with the mares.

'We've got him, Jake!' Blaine muttered on an intake of breath.

'Seems like it, boss,' the cowman answered.

Jim, aware of sudden fear catching at his heart, made no

comment. He thought, as he looked at the stallion, that he was gazing upon an animal soon to be doomed . . . not to the rope, but to death.

He could hear, way back in the depths of his mind, the stallion's cry he had heard that day of the whirlwind . . . the cry that had come winding down to him from off the heights of Wild Horse Bench: and he knew instinctively that this stallion was the very same that now stood by the river with his father's mares.

There came rising up in him then a terror for the horse he sensed would soon be taken. Mingled with that terror was a pity that was almost a betrayal of his father. He felt he must aid the stallion to escape.

A little wind, snaking across the desert, whispered in the mesquite and caused a trail of dust to mark its course. The young rancher felt that he was witnessing the end of a ghost stallion's journey. . . .

Scarcely a minute later, Jeff Blaine and Jake, were spurring their horses forward to cut off the stallion's attempt to escape.

The great round-up was on!

CHAPTER SEVENTEEN

IT WANTED but a few minutes to high noon, and it was very hot. The time and place of meeting up with the stallion had come about much as Blaine and Jake had anticipated, only it was much hotter than either had expected. The heat-waves rose in quivering veils across the river. On the eastern bank, another wisp of wind had caused a slight dust-haze to rise; and racing through it, heading due north, was the Pahute stallion and Blaine's four mares. The animals were moving with a burst of speed that was confusing, for they were following the course of the river as if intent on keeping it on their right flank as a possible means of escape should the pursuit prove too exacting.

Blaine and his men, not wishing to drive the stallion and the mares into the water, were in difficulties in making the exact pace necessary to keep the animals in view rather than overtake them.

Despite this, however, Pahute was only just holding his own. He was making no real headway, due partly to the fact that he continued to hug the river bank, and partly because the long trek he had already made was beginning to tell on him. He was, too, at a disadvantage by having to keep the mares on the move. They seemed to know that Blaine was anxious to get them away from the stallion's influence, and as if aware at last of the dangers ahead, once or twice they attempted a break-away, only to be confounded by Pahute's savage lunges at them.

Tired though he might be, the stallion was yet relentless in his efforts to retain what he had stolen and at the same time keep ahead of his pursuers. Thin, curling skeins of sand flew up behind him as he ran, and it was not until he reached a stretch of stunted cedars that his pace visibly slackened.

By now the afternoon was growing to its close, and the air began to cool a little.

Jeff Blaine, following a brief consultation with Jake, had decided to slow down a trifle, for it was obvious that the stallion was bent on making a stand inside the cedar compound as if he was aware that the dwarfed trees would aid him to withstand any concentrated attack. More than that, Blaine felt that the horse sensed that if the worse happened, there was still the river, and beyond the cedars, there was a stretch of sand reaching out into midstream. This sandbar quite clearly broke the downward flow of the water, and might prove of considerable assistance to an animal striking out for the opposite bank.

The rancher then proceeded to put into action the plan he and Jake had already decided upon. They were counting on the afterglow of the sunset streaming across the distant western mountains and turning the river into a dazzling mirror of light which might deter the stallion from entering the water to essay an escape.

With this idea therefore dominating their actions, Jake, accompanied by Jim and two others, started to ride around the cedar compound. They hoped to cut off the stallion's route north should he make a break out from his present refuge.

Jimmie was thinking that it seemed so easy. What would the stallion do when he found himself confronted by four men, all with ropes ready to round him up.

The grass and sage were scant north of the cedars, with here and there a clump of brush to break the unwinding of the river. Northwards, however, were some sandstone outcrops, all weathered into the usual monumental appearance that gave them a weird dignity, particularly in the warm gathering of the sunset.

Young Blaine had only just taken in the unexpected uprising of the monuments when he heard a distant shouting. The next instant, the four mares, hotly pursued by Pahute, came bursting out from the cedar wood.

Jake went into the attack. Swinging a rope, he gave a triumphal shout.

Pahute broke the pace he was making, rearing savagely as the mares went streaming away both left and right of him.

'We've got him!' Jake screamed.

Jim spurred his horse, moved by the excitement of the moment. He saw, dimly, that his father and the men were coming out of the wood. The next moment, the two beside him, went after the fleeing mares, shouting to him to follow.

Without any thought of disloyalty to his father, he swung his horse about and went after Jake.

The stallion was now caught between two opposing forces. Blaine and the cowhands were now well clear of the cedar compound, and Jake and Jim heading towards him.

Pahute reared again, screaming with rage. Forgotten now were the mares that had brought this dire misfortune on him. He turned and faced the river, confident of his ability to outrun those who were rapidly closing in on him.

As Blaine and Jake had supposed, the afterglow was pouring in crimson and gold across the mountains, and the light dazzled the stallion as he faced due west.

There was no other avenue of escape open to him. His only course was to make for the river and, despite the heavy flow of water, strike out for the opposite bank.

Then just as Jake closed in to within a dozen feet, whirling his lasso, Pahute was away, wild-eyed and screaming with terror, his tail splayed out behind him as his legs moved faster than any stallion's legs had moved before. In the short second or two that beheld Jake swinging his rope, the animal was at the river bank.

Pahute was badly alarmed at the unexpected turn of events. More than that, he was scared of the swirling river. An obscure instinct warned him of the danger that might accompany any attempt to make a crossing with the flow of water so strong. Yet another instinct, riding hard over the other, cautioned him not to submit to man. For now, in his adversity, his great ancestors were speaking to him out of the past, telling him of their own experiences with man, the destroyer of their kind. Even Diablo was there, seeming to stand at his very side. Thus his ignorance of man and what he stood for, was supplanted by the sudden knowledge that came to him on the rising of the fevered blood in his veins. In the quick, backward glance Pahute gave, he saw in both the man and the coiling thing he held the badge of betrayal, and knew that should the rope even touch him, freedom would be taken from him. . . .

Pahute plunged forward as Jake, pulling at his own animal, half-stood in the stirrups the better to throw the lasso.

Only a second was he poised thus, with Jim closing in on him, and Blaine and a couple of ranch hands riding hard to join up with him. A second only . . . and Pahute was sliding off the bank into the swirling torrent which here, at this point, was tossing and boiling as an under-current, swinging back from the sandbar, not only made the river deeper, but also more turbulent.

The rapid flowing of the torrent broke over Pahute's chest, then his legs threshed the strong undertow. He made a determined effort to strike out for the opposite bank. His eyes rolled with fear, but he kept a steady course, moving farther and farther away from the place where his would-be pursuers now stood watching him.

Then further misfortune overtook him. About seven or eight yards from the bank was a whirlpool, and despite the strenuous efforts Pahute made, he was drawn into the vortex of foaming water.

For a moment or so he was able to raise himself, his head thrust up into the air like some demon rising from the torrent. Then his body was swung around and around. No longer could he defeat the flow of the water. It had caught him in a grip as relentless as any quicksand. He felt himself being sucked deeper and deeper into its influence. He screamed out again and again, his forelegs striking the undertow in vain.

Another ten seconds of this uneven struggle and he would have been completely caught and drawn into the very centre of the whirlpool.

Jeff Blaine, however, acting more quickly and decisively than any of his men, swung his lasso, at the same time driving his horse into the river. The rope hissed over the stallion's head, the noose settling with unerring accuracy in a coil about his neck.

Meanwhile he had succeeded in turning his horse's head towards the bank, at the same time tugging with all his might at the rope which he had hitched into his saddle. He felt the backward pull as the lasso tightened, and but for the strain taken by the saddle, he would have been hauled into the river.

Jake had, by now, taken a hand in the hazardous adventure. He too had driven his horse into the river, and also, with a deft turn of hand, managed to get yet another rope over Pahute's neck. He then did exactly the same as Jeff Blaine, turning his horse in towards the bank and tugging viciously to relieve the strain on the other.

Pahute by this time began to respond to the pull to free him from the whirlpool. Fear lent strength to his threshing limbs, and he made a determined effort to break free of the influence of the remorseless suction. Aided by the two ropes and the riders who were now on the river bank, he found himself making headway at last, and was soon swimming directly towards the spot where the men were waiting for him.

For the moment, the stallion's only conscious fear was to get clear of the water that had so nearly drowned him. He had not the slightest doubt that once he was on the river bank, he could break free of the thongs about his neck and elude those who had pursued him to such a bitter end.

At last he was in that section of the river where the under-current from the distant sandbar broke and rolled over his back.

This time he found the eddying water aiding him, and within half a minute he was scrambling out on to the bank where, with the water streaming from him, he stood panting from exhaustion.

On either side of him, at about five yards distant in each case, Jeff Blaine and Jake held the ropes taut. The stallion discovered he could not move his head without causing himself a deal of distress. He attempted to rear and only succeeded in choking himself. As the breath seemed withdrawn from his lungs, he ceased his efforts and found he could thus breathe again.

Here was a new terror he had not experienced before. He could not understand what had happened to him. The men neither spoke nor moved. Those who stood a little distance away, watching, seemed vague and indistinct. Suddenly he lunged forward, and once again found the ropes tightening about his neck.

Greater terror than ever now held him in its grip. He, who till now had lived free, was free no longer!

Pahute held his head up, his eyes wild, his mouth open and his teeth gleaming. A cry, weird and terrible, came from him. A great hate and terror were expressed in it. All savagery and brutishness marked every line of his body as he stood helpless, held captive by the two ropes and the two men who sat like statues on horses that were equally as still. Had he been able to move he would have killed not only the riders but the animals who carried them. As it was, he could only stand very still, trembling, and conscious of the terrible fear that brought weakness to his legs and a spasmodic beat to his heart. . . .

Then he heard a voice . . . a man's voice saying agonizingly: 'Let him go, Dad. . . . Oh, please set him free. . . .'

Something deep down inside him compelled the stallion to look at the young man who had spoken thus: and so might Diablo, his distant ancestor, have looked when the Apache Chieftain, his master, once said 'Diablo, you devil horse, because you could have killed me, and did not, I set you free. . . .' Indeed, the voice of the Apache might have been the voice of the young man. The stallion would not have known otherwise. All he did seem to understand was that it held a sound he seemed to know, yet could not have known because he had not, till this fateful day, encountered man. . . .

Even as the vague remembrance gathered strength in his pulsing blood, so did another voice strike an even greater note of familiarity . . . for this time, it was the age-old note of authority which even those, who inhabit the wild, had known and feared from time immemorial. . . .

Jeff Blaine merely remarked: 'Let him go? Not this one. I'll either break him or kill him. This son of Blue Streak will now learn who is his master.'

Jim sat mute, not recognizing in his father's voice the tones of a man who was usually so kind and considerate, particularly to animals.

He stared, unbelieving. It was most extraordinary . . . that sight of an all-wild horse held captive between two men who sat so still and unperturbed.

The stallion's head was thrust forward in a gesture of hate, the mouth agape, ready to bite and kill.

But Jim sensed that the Pahute stallion would belong to no one.

*   *   *   *   *

The afterglow died slowly in the west, and the light went from the river. As the first stars came out, two men, riding with great difficulty towards the dwarf cedars, hauled between them a reluctant stallion whose eyes were blinded by the terror he felt, and whose legs trembled with every step he was forced to take.

It was as though, in this, his greatest hour of need, those from whom he had sprung, had deserted him, and now stood afar off witnessing his deep humiliation and defeat. There was, for the time being, no fight left in him. The ropes about his neck with the constant threat of throttling him, had done what no man with a whip could have done. Yet, beyond the fear and terror lay what remained of his past dignity. It would sustain him in his worst hours, and one day, possibly, bring him back to that freedom which he had lost.

An hour later, that same stallion, securely held by a stake, stood miserably listening to the far off cry of a coyote and the not so distant murmur of the river. Less than twenty yards away, hobbled to keep them from straying, were other horses, and the four mares Pahute had driven from the ranch under the Santa Rosa Mountains.

An eagle, late in the sky, and uncertain because the night was nigh come and the last light rapidly fading, hung where a a blush of crimson still lingered. Then as if to guide him to his distant eyrie, one spearhead of light leapt athwart those mountains of the west.

The bird swung about in the sky and hovered for a brief moment longer. His harsh, lonely cry, echoed eerily through the evening hush, reaching the ears of Pahute who just shivered. Again the cry came to him, floating away . . . fading as did the spearhead of light that was guiding the eagle home.

So, for the stallion, began a very long, and terrifying night.

CHAPTER EIGHTEEN

AT LONG last, the stars went out one by one, and the
questing coyotes uttered their final cry before making
for their lairs. There was then a brief hour or so of indeterminate
gloom, followed by the kindling of the dawn. The daylight
was like an invading army, advancing slowly from the east,
bringing shape to the desert, and a distorted identity to the
scrub and cedars. In the end, colour had taken place of
greyness, and when the sun came up, the river sparkled and
sang its timeless song, and a blue bird—a stranger to these
parts—took up temporary lodging in one of the cedars close
to where Pahute stood in utter dejection.

The camp was early astir. Soon a fire was burning and the
smell of cooking mingled with that of wood smoke. The other
horses moved in closer towards the camp and the men sitting
around the fire. The stallion watched, not understanding their
close affinity with man, and after a while, lost interest, and
resumed his brooding.

Suddenly he became alert. The young fellow who had spoken
to the older man the previous evening, stood within a dozen
feet of him. He was looking at him with sadness. For the first
time Pahute did not flinch at the nearness of one whom he
regarded as an enemy. This man had not used the rope on
him, and the stallion could see that he still did not possess
such an instrument of torture.

Then a queer thing happened. The young man began to
speak, softly, and with a certain musical note in his voice.
The stallion had no way of understanding what was being said
to him, had no knowledge whatever of the use to which words
could be put. All he did know was that he had no immediate
reaction of fear. His terror had gone from him. Moreover,

that remnant of dignity, smouldering beneath the shame of captivity, began to flicker and burn a little more strongly because of the man who stood so near to him and who made no attempt whatever to menace him and bring him further shame.

The dejected appearance that had characterized his entire attitude since being hauled from the river, was no longer evident. He had managed to live through the long night, and now, with the dawn, this man had come, bringing not further tribulation, but an odd, indefinable measure of companionship.

Had Pahute but known it, it was the blood of Diablo that was telling him not to fear but to try and understand . . . Diablo who had served man and finally gained from him freedom and peace.

Then Pahute felt himself once again betrayed. The older man was approaching. Before the stallion could turn with anger to face this other, the younger man was speaking in a different tone of voice. The words he uttered were no longer addressed to the horse.

'Let him go, Dad,' Jim was saying. 'Take him down to the sandbar where he can cross the river with safety and set him free.'

Although Jeff Blaine was in a less dogmatic mood after a night's sleep, and no longer wished the stallion any injury, he yet could not bring himself to set the horse free. As he saw it, the animal was far too fine a creature to wander the wild. In the morning light, he looked splendid, and Blaine told his son so.

'If we manage to break him in, he'll make the finest horse in all the west,' he said.

The rancher could not keep the note of pride out of his voice. He could almost see the future then—this magnificent animal broken to the saddle, and his, Jeff Blaine's, own horse. How proud a man could be, sitting athwart that straight back, feeling the rhythm and movement of muscles with every step the animal took, and knowing that he was controlling that rhythm and movement merely by the use of hands firmly guiding the reins.

In that brief instant that the rancher's mind had jumped from the present to the future, the stallion started to paw the ground angrily, and snorting with rising anger, showed only too clearly that he had recovered from his terror of the previous night, and now was prepared to fight with all his might to resist the final humiliation . . . that of being subservient to man.

Jimmie had stepped back at the first sign of Pahute's growing anger, and then remarked to his father: 'See, you might as well let him go. He'll fight you to the very end!'

But Jeff Blaine would fight just as hard, harder in fact, for now the pride of possession was rising up in him, and even had he the wish, he could not now let the stallion go.

His eyes turned from the horse to his son.

'Jim,' he said with utter finality in his tones, 'I'm not going to let him return to the wild. No sir! I'm going to break him in if it's the last thing I do. . . .'

With which remark, Blaine turned away and hastened back to the camp to prepare for his first serious assault on the unwilling stallion.

*   *   *   *   *

There then began the long and terrible struggle for mastery. Over and over again did the rancher try to subdue the stallion's spirit, keeping him on the end of the rope and dragging him after his own horse into the desert. Both Jimmie and Jake accompanied them to ensure that the stallion did not suddenly go mad and rush the rancher.

There were occasions when Pahute seemed likely to do just that, and they were marked by his great obstinacy when he stood with feet firmly planted in the sand, refusing to move.

When he did go into action, it was to make a quick and vicious lunge in the direction of his tormenter, but by brilliant displays of horsemanship, Jeff Blaine always managed to elude the stallion's most desperate attacks, often swinging about so rapidly that Pahute was all but thrown off his feet.

So it went on for almost a week, and by this time, Pahute hated the smell of man more than he did that of mountain lions. He had, however, lost all fear. He was what he had been before man had captured him—a wild horse that would never give in.

Now that he had got to understand the ways of man and his subtle acts of guile when opposed, the stallion found that humiliation at his loss of freedom was completely replaced by a hatred so overwhelming that he grew more and more cunning as day succeeded day.

At the end of a week's persistent struggle to make the stallion recognize him as his master, Jeff Blaine acknowledged that for the time being at least, he was defeated in his efforts. The horse had become even wilder and more determined in his efforts to resist, and the rancher began to wonder if perhaps it wouldn't be best after all to let the animal go.

Unfortunately for Pahute, when the rancher found himself thinking thus, some particularly striking attitude of his roused once again the man's deep admiration for the horse, and fanned the desire to subdue him. And so, the uneven struggle would be commenced all over again, and respite only came when Blaine felt he must return home, and ordered his men to break camp.

Jeff Blaine consulted Jake as to the best means of making the stallion tag along without the usual struggle which always accompanied any effort calculated to make the horse gallop.

'Best let us both have ropes on him,' Jake suggested. 'With us ridin' ahead of him, and keepin' him steady, he'll just have to follow. He certainly won't find it over easy to buck against two ropes. . . .'

Blaine acknowledged the logic of such advice, wondering secretly if, at some time or other, his cowman hadn't been an experienced horse wrangler.

That the advice was sound in action was obvious when the rancher and his party set off eastwards. Pahute, securely held by two ropes, found that his refusal to follow resulted in his being almost throttled.

At the end of what seemed little more than a journey of terror for the horse, Pahute found himself prisoner in a corral adjacent to the ranch house under the Santa Rosa Mountains.

Here, for the first time since his capture, he was set free of the hated rope.

For the whole of the first day in the corral, Pahute stood in the centre of the corral, moving little more than a pace at a time. By sundown, he was still in much the same position as when the rope had been taken from his neck.

Then as night came, a soft, velvet night falling from off the mountains, with the air delightfully cool after the heat of the day and the stars shining large and bright over the unfenced lands, Pahute ranged back and forth. He lifted each leg slowly and with a delicacy that was born of uncertainty and suspicion. Soon he came to understand that he could indeed move unhampered from one end of the corral to the other, and as this discovery changed into confidence, he started to race around the enclosure, running faster and faster with every step he took.

He continued this constant round until dawn made pink the sky, and he only ceased when sounds of life came from the bunk house and the ranch itself.

That day, he was tossed bundles of hay by Jim who tried again and again to make him eat. The stallion refused to touch anything. He was more suspicious than ever. Never before had he been given food. Even since his capture, he had managed to eat off the grass where he had been tethered.

He eyed Jim angrily, and tossed his head, backing away to the far side of the corral.

It was not until late in the afternoon that he was again subjected to the rope and made to run round and round at Blaine's bidding, while Jake, whooping and shouting, encircled the corral from the outside.

By nightfall, the stallion was weary of the enforced exercise, and was reluctant to come to the edge of the corral for the rope to be taken from his neck.

Blaine mis-interpreted the horse's manner. Standing at what he considered was a safe distance away, he took the stallion's hesitation as the first sign of submission, and was in an elated mood when he went in for his supper. Soon, he thought, Pahute would be less aggressive and thus easy to handle.

Not long afterwards, as another night drew a curtain of purple over the unfenced lands, the stallion ranged once more, edging his way cautiously around the corral, testing every stake and seeking for a weak part in the structure that was exceptionally high. When he found that he could never hope to kick through the stakes as he did on that other occasion, he bucked, lunged and wheeled in silent anger.

It wanted but an hour to daybreak when Pahute stood like a shadow in the very centre of the enclosure, listening to the near hooting of two owls. So still was the horse that one of the birds flew low over his head before the creature realized that it was a living thing that stood there.

Generations of knowledge were stirring in Pahute then. His feet seemed planted so firmly in the ground that he was almost part of the very earth itself. From it he seemed to be absorbing strength. His head, set in a westerly direction, pointed the way he desired to go—to freedom. His eyes gleamed, his nostrils flared. The longer he stood firmly emplanted in the very centre of the corral, the more did he feel a strange power and strength surging up in him. His eyes, bridging the gloom, saw clearly the copse, black against the skyline, saw too a scattering of rocks back of the shack that housed hens. Then again an owl hooted. The second bird flew over the corral and away into the east where the first light of a new day was already flickering like a furnace below the horizon.

The bird's silent flight had focused the stallion's attention on the tall fence that surrounded him. The strength he seemed to be garnering from the earth beneath his feet surged up more strongly than ever. There was a tightening in his leg joints, a slow lift to his tail. The next instant the stallion was racing towards the fence that Blaine said no horse could ever hope to leap.

In the very act of running, his body spread out, lengthened. Then without any hesitation in the stride he had so carefully paced from the centre of the corral, he went sailing over the fence . . . sailing over in a long, soaring leap that had the appearance of carrying him up to the very skies and then down to a light, easy landing. . . .

No sound issued from him as he came to rest some yards from the corral, no grunt, no gasp. Neither did he stumble. His balance was superb. Then he was away like the wind, heading direct for the copse, running at an incredible speed, his strides like the quick movements of one who, at last, had gained that upon which his heart had been set these many days.

Nothing could stop him now. He had no thought of the mares, only of getting clear away from the ranch. The ground rolled from beneath his feet at the pace he set, then he was through the copse, now becoming grey with the approaching dawn, and was soon heading for the first of the unfenced country.

His mane tossed over his head, his tail streamed out behind him. He was first on the earth, then in the air . . . a racing shadow that had known captivity and now was free . . . a ghost horse intent on reaching the mountains of the west where man was not known, and only the wind made murmuring sounds in the evening hush and freedom was part of the hills and the sky far above them.

Pahute's heart beat firmly as he ran, and only the sun coming up behind him, witnessed him racing round the ridge of rocks that had been instrumental in bringing about his humiliation. When at last the sun shone like a burnished shield in the freshwater pond, the stallion had long since vanished, and the horizon was but a shimmering heat haze, with no shadow on it, and no life. . . .

It was a lovely, calm day.

Book Four
Ghost Horse of the Oregon Trail

CHAPTER NINETEEN

AT THE time when the Pahute stallion went on the rampage, the golden age of wild horse legend was nigh past, the records being full of such names as the 'Pacing White Stallion, Diablo, Dark Fury, Blue Streak, Silver Star and Star Face— the great thief of the Cimmaron. Only with certain of the Indian tribes did further names sound familiar. The feuding Cheyennes and Commanches at one time found a common source for raids in a band of horses led by a big bay.

Then the Cheyennes, in an unexpected round-up, finally captured the bay. For a while after the event this particular horse's name began to possess some significance until at the heel of the year, in Colorado, a party of Kiowas made a raid on a neighbouring tribe, and among the captured horses secured a jet black stallion said to be a son of Dark Fury. Even he, however, was spoken of for a short while only, then became, like so many other animals, lost in legendary conjecture.

Meanwhile, in Nevada, Blue Streak still held respect among many wranglers, and was reputed to head a herd of more than a hundred animals.

The east, unfortunately, was fast invading the west. The Buffalo herds were quickly vanishing, and with them, the wild horse herds went farther and farther into the mountain fastnesses of the west.

It was about this time that Idaho, Nevada and Oregon, were the last strongholds of the mustang and the surviving members of the better class horse said to have sprung from the original Spanish strains.

Old-timers shook their heads and mourned the passing of a life that, for them, had been full of adventure and colour.

Only one truly great horse stood out now where, but a few years before, there had been many. When Blue Streak went, the wranglers said the last of the great horses would go with him, for to them, he *was* the last.

Then in a blaze of rumour and greatly exaggerated story-telling, the name of Pahute—the Ghost Hoss—swept like wild-fire from the ranch lands of Nevada to Oregon, penetrating even to California. The wranglers gleefully told themselves that the old days were not quite dead. Many of them formed bands to hunt out the stallion's stronghold, but like his sire, Blue Streak, the Ghost Hoss was hard to trail, and a deal harder to find. He had apparently learnt his lesson from his raid on Jeff Blaine's ranch.

Even so, after that, not a rancher south of the Nevada—Oregon State Line could claim immunity from his daring raids. What was most surprising in the circumstances was that Jeff Blaine himself, in time, lost some of his yearlings, although he still retained his four brood mares.

Blaine was the one man expected to know most about the great blue-black stallion with the white mane and tail. It was an old story now—that of the trek he had made to recapture his mares, and how, with them, he had taken the stallion. It was also a much discussed tale of what subsequently followed when the stallion escaped.

Jake, Blaine's cowman, and Jim Blaine, with a couple of ranch hands, had set off to trail the stallion once more. They had lost it at the Quinn River. Since the river was no longer in spate, it was assumed that the horse had made a safe crossing which had not been possible on that other occasion when he had Blaine's mares with him.

The men then hit the trail southwards to Wild Horse Bench, but no sign of the horse, or indeed of any living animal, could they discover in this most ancient of wild horse strongholds.

Because fresh water seemed scarce in the locality, it was generally agreed that the wild horse had long since given up using the mountain, and as a result, Wild Horse Bench was ruled out as a likely hiding place for either Pahute, or his sire, Blue Streak.

What lent support to the theory that neither stallion worked the range and desert Badlands east of the Pine Forest range, was the fact that such round-ups as were made on ranches were all in the region of the Oregon State Line, or more farther south, beyond Pahute Peak.

It was old Colorado Ted who finally set the boundaries, and from his remarks, indicating that Blue Streak was operating in the south and his son more in the north, sprang the ranging areas explored by wranglers.

Searches were therefore made for Blue Streak in the valleys and canyons adjacent to Division Peak, and the land-locked river east of the main mountain group. The searches for Pahute, the Ghost Horse, were made along the border territories, nobody realizing that Blue Streak was operating from Red River Canyon, his old summer grazing ground, and Pahute from Wild Horse Bench which he had reached a month after Jake and Jim Blaine had visited it and declared the outcrop to be completely uninhabited by any wild horse band.

Within a year of his escape from Jeff Blaine's corral, the name of Pahute as the 'Ghost Hoss' was as widely known as that of his sire. Many of his raids were carried out under the very noses of the ranchers, but nobody actually witnessed him making the assaults. His movements over the unfenced lands were quick and silent, and always carried out within a reasonable distance of the Quinn River. How he got the yearlings he stole across the river was a mystery. Whilst many ranch hands could claim to having trailed the stallion to the river itself, nobody could discover any trace of him on the other side. Some asserted that the stallion never crossed the river. Others that he drove the animals he had stolen into the river and made them swim upstream, thus making it doubly certain that nobody could trail him.

Jake and Jim were often puzzled by what they heard. Finally both came to the conclusion that Pahute must indeed have a hide-out up among the foothills below Split Peak. There could be no other reasonably safe place as far as they could see. Wild Horse Bench never once occurred to them. It was, according to the many tales that were told, too far south.

Like all other ranchers and mustangers, Jake and the Blaines were in complete ignorance of the recently opened corridor through the mountains, leading to the area of volcanic waterholes where Pahute had formed his herd.

Even had they been aware of its existence, they would not have conceived any stallion driving mares and yearlings through it, and then down along the desolate volcanic territory between the Pine Forest range and the eastern foothills. That this was a hide-out in every sense of the word was manifest by the use to which it was put by Pahute.

Like Blue Streak, Pahute had an uncanny sense of direction, coupled now with a cunning sharpened by his recent experiences with man. Before setting out on the rampage, the stallion thoroughly surveyed the whole area of his anticipated activities, and it was only when he was assured that horses were grazing in bunches, and seldom visited by the ranchers and stockmen, that he made his round-ups.

*   *   *   *   *

For three years, following his escape from Jeff Blaine's corral, Pahute lived in isolation in the mountain fastnesses of Wild Horse Bench, and each evening, when the western sun flamed and died over the Pine Forest ridge, he stood on the caprock, gazing down upon the dreaded Black Rock Desert and the distant water basin of the Quinn. Always too, at sundown, as if it were a ritual with him, he would rear and paw at the stars, and then, and then only, did he send his whinnying cry echoing out across the desert.

GHOST HORSE

Many old-timers following the trail along the Quinn heard the echo of it, and could never tell from which point it came. Since Wild Horse Bench was now considered an absolutely deserted mountain outcrop, nobody ever thought of visiting it. Even when these same old-timers met others on the trail, and spoke of the scream at sunset, all agreed, with shaking heads, that it was but an echo carried down from the north on the high surface winds . . . a cry, without a doubt, of the Ghost Hoss who not only ranged the northern borderlands, but also led the long dead mustangs along the unfenced rangelands of the sky. . . .

Thus grew the legend of Pahute, now always referred to as the Ghost Horse. Like his sire, Blue Streak, he was reputed to have been seen in most any place west of Idaho and Utah. Frontiersmen saw him ranging the Shoshone Mesa way down below Antelope Creek: others saw him with great bands of mustang, fleeing the onslaught of wranglers from as far away as the Columbia River to the Rio Grande.

It was always the same tale they told . . . of a blue-black hoss, with white mane and tail . . . faster than any other hoss seen before . . . as big as Blue Streak, as black, at times, as the fabled Diablo.

Always was it the Ghost Horse they saw. None other: and if half the tales that were told could be accepted as true, the stallion ranged most of the western states, and was in as many places at the same time as there were wranglers trailing wild horses. Wherever there were herds, such were led by the Ghost Hoss. Not a night passed but his cry roused wranglers from their camp-fires only to see in the sky a racing, tossing herd of phantom horses, all led by the great Ghost who screamed and thrashed his way through the clouds until the dawn came and drove him and his bands into the fastnesses of unknown horizons. . . .

Perhaps of all the tales that were told, one was indeed true. It came from a couple of wranglers who had been driven to shelter from a storm in the area of High Rock Lake, west of Pahute and Division Peaks.

The whole mountain ranges were heavy in mist, and the harsh heat of an exceedingly dry summer had been broken by a freak storm that had lasted for over four days. According to the wranglers, nothing quite like it had ever been seen before in those parts. That it was very bad indeed over the mountains was obvious from the sullen drum-like thuds of thunder that went on and on, echoing repeatedly from peak to peak. There was water everywhere, pouring down the scarred cliffs, filling the desert sinks and turning the innumerable alkali slush creeks into deceptive lakes.

The wranglers found sufficient covering for themselves and their horses within the shelter of an enormous scattering of rocks that broke the force of the torrential rain.

It was just after the fifth day when the storm had rolled away northwards that they saw a scene they were never likely to forget. Approaching from both north and south were two huge herds of wild horses, each herd being led by a blue-black stallion. The only noticeable difference in the two leaders was that the animal leading the band from the south possessed a snowy white mane and tail, while the other was just blue-black, but with the same identical white stockings that characterized the legs of the other.

Both men knew that they were gazing upon the two most famous stallions of that time—Blue Streak, and his son, the Ghost Hoss. Neither animal showed any animosity towards the other as they led their respective bands to the grazing around High Rock Lake. This was all the more remarkable since there were many mares in both herds, and a considerable number of colts.

It was almost as though driven by the terrible storm from their different mountain strongholds, both stallions adopted a neutral attitude towards each other. There could be no doubt whatever that neither stallion was going to challenge the right of the other to the use of the grazing and the waterholes adjacent to the lake.

Perhaps, in adversity, they realized that there was greater safety in numbers; perhaps neither felt the need to fight for further possessions. Each herd was much larger than usual, and doubtless difficult to control as a result.

The outcome of this strange and completely unexpected gathering of two enormous bands of wild horses was that never in their lives before had the two wranglers seen so many horses at one time, and certainly never, till then, seen either Blue Streak or the Ghost Hoss.

Since they were not in any position to attempt a round-up of either stallion, the wranglers could only remain closely hidden in their rocky enclosure, watching for three whole days the great gathering of what they considered must have been the finest 'hoss flesh in the entire west'.

For most of the time, the stallions stood away off, surveying the mares, from what had, for them, become a vantage point.

With the storm gone and the sky clear again, the lake became a blue that afforded a sharp contrast with the fresh green of the grass and the red and grey rocks. The sage had a hint of purple in it, and the long stretches of sand flaming orange-red on the edge of the green, gave the whole scene an air of unreality, while both north and south, the long, fanged peaks still smoked where cloud seemed caught and held in sinuous fingers that refused to let them go.

Some whooper swans, come in from the east, were in possession of a strip of land that thrust out into the lake, and they gleamed white in the sunlight, and where a few alders draped the water's edge, a couple of mocking birds called to one another for most of the day.

Heedless of everything but the grass beneath their feet, the two wild horse herds moved from place to place, feeding and lazing away the hours, while the colts played and the two stallions watched. . . .

Only very occasionally did Pahute and Blue Streak round up the strays, and then always with regard to avoiding any attempt at a stampede.

Thus, the one and only meeting of Blue Streak and his son, neither approaching too closely to the other, neither showing the slightest sign of aggressive action.

Then, when the moon was riding full over the mountains of the east, without the slightest sign or warning of what was taking place, both stallions got their respective herds on the move. Pahute went south through the pass of the very mountain massif on which he had been born, and Blue Streak due north, passing around the nearby foothills towards Summit Lake that sign-posted the way to Red River Canyon.

There was no unexpected stampede as might well have happened when two large and completely alien herds of horses were set on the move, no whinnying cries to tell the wranglers what was happening. The leaders worked quietly and efficiently, and when the dawn came, no sign of any horse marked the recent grazing site.

On the fourth morning, the two wranglers rubbed the sleep out of their eyes and looked at each other in amazement. But for the droppings and innumerable hoof marks, there was nothing at all to tell that the evening before, two great bands of wild horses, together with two of the finest stallions in the west, had been centred around High Rock Lake.

When a couple of weeks later, they had succeeded in crossing the Quinn and hit old Jeff Blaine's ranch, their story was completely disbelieved. Nothing like it had ever been told before.

Only when old Colorado Ted made his annual visit to the area late in the fall and heard the same tale, did he nod his hoary head in agreement.

He was quite the oldest man Jim Blaine had ever set eyes on, tanned and wizened by sun, wind and rain, and toughened by the many years he had known. His clothes were in keeping with the rest of him, being those of a trapper familiar in an age now past.

Despite his years, Colorado Ted was yet a man whose word was much respected throughout the west, and when he said that it was perfectly true that Blue Streak and the Ghost Hoss had been seen together, nobody disputed the fact any longer.

There was much wisdom in the old man's voice when he said: 'Yep! I spied them two hosses mesself, comin' down from off the mountains when the storm was real bad. Seemed to me at the time that they hadn't long met, but because the weather was bad in them hills, they had a sort of truce between 'em. I've knowed it happen before. . . . A coupla of bears it was that time. . . . Still. . . .'

It was Jimmie, however, who asked what mountains the old man had been on at the time of the storm.

Ted looked at him gravely, and then shook his head.

'I don't rightly remember,' he answered, uttering the lie with all innocence in his eyes. 'I only knowed I spied 'em, but whether I was on the north trail or the one farther south, I just don't recall. . . .'

He paused for a moment as if pondering the matter. Then he said: 'I do know that I was somewhere near the Quinn when I saw one of 'em alone. . . .'

'Which one?' Jimmie asked breathlessly.

'Aw . . . 't' was the Ghost Hoss, I reckon. He was standing on a butte in the moonlight. Yep! I spied him plain that night. His white tail an' mane was givin' out a glow like he was a hoss on fire. . . .'

'Not dead?' Jimmie asked.

Colorado Ted smiled.

'Nope! 'E ain't dead, that one. Nor is Blue Streak. They be still the great hosses o' the west.'

Jimmie Blaine exulted at the old man's words. One day . . . one day soon, mebbe, he'd hit the trail again, just to see the Ghost Hoss once more. . . .

CHAPTER TWENTY

Pahute's long stay in the area of Wild Horse Bench had done much to give him more than a mere superficial knowledge of the surrounding country. He knew every trail across the desert, and particularly those occasionally frequented by wranglers. Since those trails used by wranglers and the like were few and far between, and used but two or three times a year, the stallion had no fear of them. He often trod those same trails himself, but always taking care that it was at a time when the winds were coming in strongly from either the north or the west, and his footprints thus blotted out by the constantly shifting sand.

*   *   *   *   *

The winter that year was mild. Although there were heavy falls of snow, none of it lay for long, save on those distant peaks that marked the north-western horizon. Then again—quite suddenly so it seemed to Pahute—it was spring again—by far the loveliest he had ever known. Not that he appreciated its beauty. He was only aware of the mildness of the atmosphere when tested from the caprock on Wild Horse Bench, and the fragrantly cool winds that came down from the north.

All in all, Pahute, the son of Blue Streak, now better known as the Ghost Horse was glad to be alive: and with the increasing measure of his days so increased the measure of his fearlessness.

Then came the hour when Pahute, in common with all other creatures of the wild, experienced his greatest period of restlessness. He became more daring in his wanderings, more insistent in his distant journeys to the Quinn River basin and his brief visits to the unfenced lands on the eastern bank.

Finally, like a challenger to the authority of man, and to Jeff Blaine in particular, Pahute set off once more in the direction of the ranchlands under the shadow of the Santa Rosa Mountains. Maybe it was the spring in his blood that urged him to go . . . maybe some vague, tantalizing remembrance of those four brood mares of Blaines that somehow, he now realized he still coveted.

Despite this, the stallion was taking no undue risk. Since he was familiar with the general terrain over which he must travel, he knew exactly where to exercise extreme caution and where it would be most prudent to move only under cover of darkness.

Resulting from this acutely developed awareness of danger, the greater part of Pahute's long trek eastward was undertaken at night. He then galloped easily under the stars, running swiftly with little noise over the sand and enjoying every moment of it.

Indeed, almost as if he had consciously willed it, he came once more to the fresh water pond in the grey half-light that preceded daybreak. The sun was still no more than a glimmering flame when he tentatively surveyed Blaine's unfenced lands before hiding up amidst the rocks below the escarpment that kept guard over this oasis of water.

Pahute did not move in towards the copse surrounding the ranch house until very late that same night. When he did so, he made no sound, and entered the security of the trees like the ghost horse he was reputed to be.

Because the night was inclined to be very warm, Jeff Blaine had left the mares in a corral that had, in the corner farthest from the ranch house, a sizeable lean-to intended to act as a stable if circumstances demanded it.

An old setter dog that had been out hunting over the unfenced lands, came up close to the copse where Pahute was hidden. Then, aware of sudden hunger, he made off abruptly in the direction of the bunk house where his sudden barking brought Jake hastening to the door. There was a sudden spilling of yellow lamplight into the darkness as the cowman let the dog in, followed by what appeared to be a deeper gloom when the door was closed again.

By midnight, it was very silent. The sky was bright with stars and the stallion, emboldened by the stillness, moved from his refuge under the trees. Treading stiff-legged, with head thrust forward and his nostrils widely flared, he approached the place where once he had suffered the degradation of captivity. Once again, he was little more than a shadow, his feet making no sound as he came up to the corral.

The mares had got his scent and were restless. All four were close to the lean-to, but as if impelled by some irresistible force, drew near to the small wicket gate that opened on to the newly-made ash path leading to the main ranch buildings.

Dark though it was, they had glimpsed Pahute, recognizing him instantly. They paused apprehensively, their eyes dilated, and their nostrils opening and closing as they sought in the only way they knew to determine the nature of the mood that had brought him to the ranch. Then instinctively, as if acting for their self-preservation, they pressed close together, flank against flank, their heads high, their ears sharply erect in nervous inquiry.

Even as they stood thus, Pahute moved swiftly around the corral and halted within the deep shadow of the lean-to. It was by the merest chance that he discovered the wicket gate that was kept fastened by the flimsiest of catches. As he pressed against the gate to peer into the corral, he felt it move slightly.

He then uttered a short whine, and the mares responded at once. They came immediately towards him.

Pahute thrust his head forward to sniff them, setting his feet firmly on the recently laid ash path. His hind legs, thrusting his body forward at an angle, brought additional pressure to bear upon the gate. Suddenly it gave beneath the concentrated weight of chest and pushing legs.

An instant later, Pahute was in the corral with the mares who, becoming excited, stepped back restlessly.

The stallion, however, did not harass them. He had no wish to set them pounding around the corral. He sought, first, to gain their trust.

With this objective in view, he moved quietly around the corral, investigating every corner, and testing every support. Then for some minutes he stood as—on that other memorable occasion he had stood—absolutely motionless and once more as black as a shadow. No owl was there this time to fly in winnowing flight over his head. There was nothing but the dark shapes of the ranch buildings, and above him, the bright stars, winking restlessly like the beat of his heart.

The mares, meanwhile, had not moved from the place where he had left them. They were nervously awaiting his next move.

At last they beheld him swinging about swiftly, but still noiselessly. He came towards them in slow, prancing steps, halting within a couple of yards. There was now, quite clearly, a definite object in his quiet manoeuvring. He wanted the mares to accept his presence at close quarters. With this one desire dominating his actions, he remained very still, merely thrusting his head forward to sniff them gently.

Still, no sound came from the ranch house, nor yet from the other buildings. The whole place was wrapped in utter silence.

At last, Pahute prepared to make the round-up. He swung away from the mares, going around in a complete circle before coming back in their direction.

A star fell in a trail of luminous light over the Santa Rosa Mountains. Away off in the night, a night bird called and a coyote set up a distant howling.

At the sound of the coyote's call, the mares closed in about the stallion for protection. They felt the stallion's body move past them towards the gap where the wicket gate had been, and there was no hesitation on their part. All four, swayed by the desire for protection against the night, went with Pahute through the gap, and so towards the copse and the trail that led west to the unfenced lands and the wild horse country beyond the unwinding of the Quinn River.

CHAPTER TWENTY-ONE

Pahute had a long memory when it came to events that, in the past, had brought him close to disaster. Moreover, he had no illusions as to the invincibility of man.

He therefore lost no time in putting as great a distance between himself and the ranch as was possible. He kept the mares running quickly, not stopping once throughout the remaining hours of darkness.

When the sun came up, and a quick glance back along the trail disclosed no sign of pursuit, the stallion was still not reassured. He recalled how rapidly he had once before been overtaken, and after allowing the mares but a very short respite, had them on the move again. Profiting from his earlier experiences, he swung away from the western trail as soon as he struck rocky ground.

He then headed the mares due south, driving them through scattered stretches of scrubland that gave camouflage to the surrounding scene, and helped to conceal the movement from those who might be following across the unfenced lands in the east.

Pahute kept up the pace, instinctively aware that the scrub was aiding him to escape detection. By sundown, he had brought the weary mares to a loop of the Quinn River that here bordered Desert Valley.

Realizing that the mares were exhausted and in need of rest, he permitted them to graze on the coarse pasture betwixt the scrub and the river basin while he, himself, kept constantly on the watch. When later that night, a keen wind came driving down from the north, the stallion went back a little way along the trail. Reaching a place where a perceptible rise in the desert floor might prove a vantage point from which to test the wind for scent, Pahute stood motionless for the best part of thirty minutes, searching every varying scent for the man-taint, but there was nothing to give rise to anxiety.

By striking the hard ground south, he had adopted a wise course. He was, for the time being at least, safe from pursuit.

Next morning before the sun came up, Pahute drove the mares across the loop of the river, and a week later, after once again fording the higher reaches of the Quinn in the Black Rock Desert area, the mares, and the stallion himself, were safely concealed in the narrow canyons of Wild Horse Bench.

*   *   *   *   *

Without the slightest doubt, Jeff Blaine had been utterly misled by Pahute's cunning. He was forced to admit defeat when they finally pitched camp west of Rebel Creek. Not even Jake, with all his trail-following experience, could pick up any sign of either the stallion or the mares.

Next morning, Jeff Blaine held a conference. All expressed the utmost surprise at their failure to find some trace of the stallion, and were just as mystified as Jake.

Even Jim, who usually had so much to say, had little to add to the others' remarks. His father little realized that it was for a reason entirely different from those already put forward.

The rancher was, none the less, far from satisfied that nothing further could be done, saying forcibly that the stallion must hide up some place or other, and where *he* was, there too were his mares.

It was then his son made the only real contribution to the discussion. He suggested that maybe, it would be a good idea if he and Jake scouted around for a bit, and then reported back to the ranch.

Jeff Blaine, secretly worried at being absent from the ranch, thought it a good enough plan to warrant his serious consideration.

He brooded over it until mid-day, then consulted Jake.

The idea appealed to the cowman, and soon afterwards, Blaine agreed to Jim and Jake continuing with the search while he and the others returned to the ranch.

So hasty had been the party's departure from the ranch that supplies had been the last consideration, and as a result, were not over plentiful. Even so sufficient was made available to last the two men for a week at least.

Such was the beginnings of the plan Jeff Blaine hoped would rid the range of the Ghost Horse. As the rancher saw it, no matter the cost, the stallion had to be found and slain! While he lived, the horse would be a persistent menace to all those ranchers and stockmen who depended on the unfenced lands for the raising of their animals.

The rancher was in a smugly optimistic mood when he finally made his home territory, and meeting up with a distant neighbour, heard that old Colorado Ted was also on the trail some place west of the Quinn.

He experienced a wave of excitement at the news.

That quick-running, thievin', no-good hoss, could not possibly escape being seen by one or other of the three men. Once his hide-out was known, his end would follow as surely as night followed day. Of this, Blaine had no doubts whatever.

So confident was he that the hand of every man was now against the stallion that he did not realize that it could be that he alone was the animal's most bitter opponent!

*   *   *   *   *

Back at Rebel Creek, in the grey light of dawn that seemed to possess an extraordinary beauty as it gathered over the desert, Jim stirred in his blanket. He suddenly sat up, and gazed at the distant outline of the Santa Rosa Mountains over which the dawn burned in indigo and red.

There was something in it that seemed to catch at his heart. He wondered if it were the beauty alone that made him feel so remote and far from reality. As he watched, he saw the morning star growing dim, and fading fast as the sinuous fingers of the dawn searched upwards.

His breath caught in his throat and a half-suppressed sigh passed his lips.

He found himself wishing that all knowledge was his, and that he could, by will alone, bridge the present and the future, and travel the many trails west where once the wagon trains rolled.

Then, as if he could no longer bear the wistful yearning in his heart, he abruptly turned his gaze to Jake.

The cowman was already awake and been watching the younger man with interest.

'What is it, Jimmie lad?' he asked kindly, not moving from the comfortable position he had made for himself.

To cover his embarrassment, Jim answered at once: 'I was just wonderin' about the Ghost Hoss.'

'What about the hoss?'

Jim shook his head. Then speaking quietly, but with a marked note of seriousness in his voice, he said: 'I'd like to tell my father that the stallion can't be found . . . nor his mares. . . .'

'That would be all right till he set out on another raid,' Jake replied. 'Then the hunt would be on again . . . next time, mebbe, with men really bent on killin'. . .'

'I suppose you're right,' Jim said with a sigh. 'But Jake, do you really want to see him caught again . . . an' this time killed, mebbe?'

'Nope. Can't say I do.'

'Can't we work out some plan?'

'It wouldn't be fair on your old man.'

'Does it matter?'

'That'd be all right, mebbe, if the hoss wasn't in Nevada

an' always on the steal. He's a rogue that one . . . every bit
as bad as Blue Streak if you ask me.'

'Then you don't think there's much we can do anyway?'

The disappointment in Jim's voice moved his companion.

'There certainly don't seem much we can do save find out
where's he hiding up,' he answered reflectively. 'That might
give us some idea as to checking him.'

'How?' he asked.

Jake shrugged his shoulders.

'I just don't know. We'd do better first to pick up some
trace of him. Point is, which way do we trek . . . north or
south?'

Jimmie was silent for a moment, lost in thought. He had
turned his gaze once more to the far off Santa Rosa Mountains.
It was at that moment that the sun came up, glowing red above
the main ridge. Night had vanished completely from the plains
and the unfenced lands. In its place, daylight was spilling like
quicksilver over the lonely wastes of the desert. Back of the
spilling light, however, were the mountains, dark against the
red and gold of the sunrise.

He saw one of the distant peaks standing out clear from the
rest of the range. It was an illusion, of course, brought into
being by the long, horizon-wide flow of light from the east.
For one brief second, that peak seemed to be spiralling up and
up, reminding the young man of another, entirely different
mountain outcrop.

He turned to Jake, exclaiming:

'Jake, let's hit the Quinn and travel south. Remember what
Colorado Ted said about seeing the Ghost Hoss on the south
trail. Supposing after all, he *is* hiding up on Wild Hoss Bench?'

The cowman rolled out of his blanket.

'Mebbe you've gotten hold of something. It could be! Yep.
It certainly could be. He could have hit the trail south by
travelling over the scrubland east o' here. . . .'

There was a kind of controlled excitement about him now.

'Jimmie boy, we'll sure make fer the Quinn and head off south to the river crossing an' Wild Hoss Bench. If you're right, and the hoss is there, mebbe we can get back the mares and call it a day. Mebbe too, we can make it darned unlikely for the hoss to trek east again. . . .'

'How?'

'By scaring him real bad. A fire of brushwood east o' the mountain might do it.'

'There ain't much brushwood as I can remember,' Jim replied.

'Ain't you the awkward one! Sure, I'd forgotten. Mebbe we'll find some way of doing it. Best get our breakfast now an' saddle up. We've a long way to go to hit that trail south to Wild Hoss Bench. . . .'

'Jake?'

Jim spoke gently, sudden misgiving bringing a sombre note to his voice.

'What?'

'You don't aim at tryin' to catch that hoss again?'

Jake shook his head, his face serious.

'Jim,' he replied, 'you an' me are pards, ain't we?' Then as the young man nodded, he went on: 'I don't aim at lettin' my pards down none. Fact is, I didn't want to catch the hoss before. It was either that I helped or see him drown in the whirlpool. . . .'

'Thanks Jake,' was all Jim said in reply.

Three [days later, the two men had forded the river at Quinn Crossing, and were soon on the south trail, with the massive shoulders of the Pine Forest Mountains dominating the entire western horizon. On the fifth day, they discovered hoof marks in the sand, and by sundown, knew for certain that they led direct to Wild Horse Bench.

The mountain lay out in the west across the undulating plain of the Black Rock Desert. It was a sharply defined silhouette of spiralling ledges, ending in the pancake shape that, in the evening light, possessed all the mystery of a gloomy castle that defied invasion by man.

That night, they were joined by Colorado Ted, a most gloomy man. He had come from the Alkali Flat country betwixt the Granite Mountains in the south and High Rock Lake, west of Pahute Peak.

He had witnessed the end of Blue Streak and his band!

*   *   *   *   *

Colorado Ted's tale was only half told when all three men were startled by what seemed an echo coming up from out of the night. They looked at each other across the flames of the camp-fire. The flickering glow on their faces emphasized the hollows beneath their cheeks and the deeper hollows where their eyes seemed turned inwards, searching not the darkness, but that innermost place within themselves where thoughts lay heavy and troubled.

The weird cry came winding across the desert from the direction of Wild Horse Bench—a cry very faint yet somehow cruelly strident. Three times it came, with no accompanying echoes. No sooner had it ceased than another call came reaching out to the men crouched over the camp-fire. It was a note of mournful significance, rising and falling in an almost musical cadence as some lone coyote mourned to the stars and gave answer to what had been a stallion's cry of defiance. . . .

CHAPTER TWENTY-TWO

THE END of Blue Streak had been as spectacular as many of the tales the old-timers had related about him. He had set out on the rampage, raiding on an extensive scale. His activities were confined for the most part to an area less than thirty miles from the nearest township where ranchers and stockmen habitually gathered. Soon the local newspaper was carrying banner headlines concerning the stallion, with almost a page devoted to what the editor called the animal's life history.

Save for the Pahute stallion, there could not be in all Utah or Nevada another horse that had the sheer audacity to carry out raids under the very noses of the men bent on his destruction.

Retribution was demanded for the damage he did and for the mares he had stolen. Then, a reward—the largest that had ever been offered for the capture of a wild horse—was circulated in every small township, and a party of experienced mustangers was got together to track down the stallion.

It was about this time that Blue Streak decided to leave the security of the Pine Forest range and blaze a trail west to High Rock Creek.

The massed movement of mares and young stock was carried out with all the stallion's usual skill. It was grand weather, with the blue sky seeming bluer than it had ever been before. There was, however, an abundance of water between the Pine Forest range and Pahute Peak, and the stallion and his herd made easy progress towards High Rock Creek and the fatal Alkali country close to the Californian border.

Blue Streak was in high spirits. He had acquired many new mares from his recent raids, and had them well under control. The whole herd was as nice a bunch of mares and young stock as could be found anywhere in wild horse country. Moreover, Blue Streak had seen to it that they had ample grazing during the long trek west.

It was a large spread of country—that country from the Californian State Line up to the Pine Forest Mountains.

The mustangers, now on the move, but with little idea as to where to locate Blue Streak, were guarding most of the waterholes, without realizing that if necessary, the stallion could go dry from four to five days without experiencing discomfort. Then some of the outriders discovered horse trails leading away westward from Summit Lake, and from that moment onwards, knowledge of the stallion's movements was no longer in doubt.

The mustangers, led by a man as tenacious as the stallion himself, began to work in relays, each small band of men moving from west to east, and from south-east to north-west in the direction of Massacre Lake and the Alkali country.

Blue Streak, still unaware that danger threatened, kept on the move, and so quietly did he carry out his activities, and so well was his herd under control, that the mustangers were completely confounded. Horse trails were evident all over the territory they covered, but there was never a sign of any animal.

Finally a Paiute Indian coming down off what was commonly known as the Wind River Mountain north of Division Peak, saw a cloud of dust hovering over the neighbourhood of High Rock Lake.

The Indian rode cautiously towards it, keeping well hidden. Within a mile or so of the lake which was fed by a river running into it from both north and south, he beheld Blue Streak and his large band of mares and yearlings.

He had no thought of any reward, but he rejoiced at the sight. Observing that the stallion who led the herd seemed intent on resting awhile in the neighbourhood, the Paiute made off with all haste for the nearest reservation of his tribe.

Three days later, with a couple of mustangers amongst them, the Indians struck High Rock Creek and found that the band of horses had moved off north.

The entire herd was following a mountain range, gulched and tumbled on its western flank and precipitous on the east, and this despite the fact that it was but an off-shoot of the hills that fell away from the main escarpment of the Pine Forest range.

Blue Streak and his band were climbing the hills at their own pace with no idea that the Paiutes were after them.

At first the Indians wondered exactly where the stallion was taking his herd. His persistent movement up the escarpment indicated that he knew exactly where he was going. Indeed such was the case. Blue Streak knew from his colthood days, that where the gulched mountains ended, there was pasture a-plenty and good watering.

Meanwhile, the days continued fair, the skies as blue as they had ever been, and the far-off vista of the green grass country that preceded the dreaded Alkali area as tantalizing as any memory of Red River Canyon. Moreover, Blue Streak was in fine fettle. Despite the fact he was no longer a young horse, he was yet strong and exceedingly healthy.

After four days on the mountain trail, Blue Streak, till then in the rear of the herd, took the lead, closely followed by some half dozen of his favourite mares.

Behind the herd rode seven Paiutes, the others having given up due to the very difficult trail. The arrangement was that the seven who now trailed the herd should drive it down to a familiar canyon east of what was known as the West Lake in the Big Lake territory.

There could be no hasty approach to the band on such a narrow, treacherous trail as that which Blue Streak followed. The ridge, of no great height, was yet becoming wilder and more broken with every mile that passed. On one side was a sheer bluff that ended in a tangled mass of rock, on the other, an equally difficult chasm that no man or horse could scale.

All in all, Blue Streak had to keep on the move. There was no place on the trail where he could rest up for the night save on the plateau a thousand feet or so above and which narrowed to a downward trail, again exceedingly narrow, that led to the lakes.

It was nigh to sunset when Blue Streak brought his band on to the plateau where he proposed resting until daybreak. Then he discovered to his horror that an Indian and one other, were on that northern trail. The Indian, one of the original band of Paiutes had acted on his own initiative, and had come up the mountain in the hope of aiding his seven companions. He had brought with him an old-timer well versed in the ways of wild horses—Colorado Ted!

To see his way blocked in such a manner, and realizing the danger of having man—his inherent enemy on the plateau with him—caused the stallion to abandon any hope he had of stopping the night on the summit. He longed to drive the men from that northern trail, and with his herd, escape to the safety of the plains below.

Having no knowledge whatever that he had been pursued, the stallion rounded up his band, determined to drive the two men from the plateau.

He was about to gallop direct at the Indian and Colorado Ted when the pursuing Paiutes came up on to the summit.

They took in at a glance the seriousness of the situation, whilst at the same time realizing that their kinsman and his companion had, in some ways, done a wise thing.

If the stallion pannicked, he and his herd were surely trapped!

The Indians brought their hard-pressed horses to a halt for a short breather. They then unhitched their ropes from their saddles.

This was the fatal mistake they made. Blue Streak would have stood firm and defied them but for the sudden glimpse of ropes which, from instinct, he hated.   —

He stood, with ears aslant, and quivering in every limb, clearly apprehensive of their next move. Perhaps ten seconds passed in that fateful pause in the life of Blue Streak. The sun was sending streamers of crimson across the western horizon. Far below, the distant lakes shone red as if with blood. The mountains north of them, stood out, sharp-edged and brutal.

Blue Streak turned his head for the briefest of moments to gaze at the two keeping guard over the northern trail.

He knew then without a doubt that the way to those lakes and mountains was securely barred to him by the Indian on the black and white mustang and that other who sat rather limply on a horse as dark as himself.

Blue Streak went into action! So too did the Indians. Head high, and facing them resolutely as they came at him, the stallion was the embodiment of all wild horses down through the ages—savage and beautiful, an animal ready to die rather than give up his freedom.

The Indians, fired with enthusiasm to capture such a lovely creature, raced towards him with grim determination to have a rope around his neck. They whooped with excitement. Their ropes cut circles in the air above them.

Then just when it seemed they must have the stallion, Blue Streak whirled around, driving his mares forward in a serried shrieking mass. Then, to the surprise of the Indians, the stallion hurled himself through their leaping ranks like a creature demented.

Whinnying with terror, the mares opened their ranks to receive him, and then turned swiftly to follow him.

All the Indians could see was the dark shape of the stallion racing through the press of the mares like a black thunderbolt, steadfast in his determination to escape the curse of the rope and the men that wielded it.

One scream only Blue Streak gave as he leapt—straight off the plateau and into space, sailing out then down . . . the herd following him to instant death on the granite crags far below.

Spasmodic screams of terror followed the terrifying death-leaps. Then there was a strange, unbroken silence, with only the blood-red sunset wavering and dying in the west, and the first star coming out. . . .

*   *   *   *   *

Thus the death of the fabled Blue Streak, Sire of the Pahute Stallion, as told by Colorado Ted.

Jim Blaine and Jake were silent. They were thinking of the Ghost Hoss out there on Wild Hoss Bench.

Did a similar fate await him and his band?

The camp-fire flickering on their faces, merely continued to etch deeply the hollows beneath their cheeks and the darker hollows beneath their eyes which, more than ever, seemed turned inwards, gazing at some distant plateau where a splendid stallion had gone to his death rather than submit to man. . . .

The night was silent, and very still. . . .

CHAPTER TWENTY-THREE

THE STAMPING of horses' hooves awoke Jim Blaine. He turned over in his blanket and stared up into the sky rosy with the dawn. The air was sharp and keen, and his first thought that he alone was awake was dispelled when he saw Colorado Ted half-bent over the camp-fire, cooking breakfast.

'Howdee, Ted!'

The old man looked up from his cooking.

'I was kinda wonderin' how long a sleep you was goin' to have . . . you an' Jake, there. . . .'

He nodded in the direction of the cowman who was still fast asleep, and snoring.

In the early morning light, Ted had a certain nobility that darkness had hidden. His eyes, old though they were, yet still had a sparkle to them, and there were moments, when suddenly darkening, they seemed to hide the great wisdom of the old-timer's mind.

Jimmie stared instinctively out across the desert at the distant pile of Wild Horse Bench. The mountain, on its eastern side, seemed a-glow with light, while the southern slopes which were barely visible from across the desert, seemed heavy with purple shadow. Wisps of cloud clung to the higher walls where the early morning sunshine appeared to stimulate an odd reflection on the pinnacled summit. The caprock itself, reared isolated above the escarpment like a dais raised to receive the King of Wild Horse Bench.

Colorado Ted, also concentrating his gaze on the distant mountain, inquired at last: 'You want to save the Ghost Hoss?'

'I do,' Jim answered at once.

The old man regarded Jim gravely.

'It won't be an easy thing to do. No sir! That one's as contrary as poor ole Blue Streak. . . .'

Ted sighed with the burden of his memories of the fabulous Blue Streak.

'Jake and I thought that mebbe we could drive him and his band away from the bench . . . mebbe over the State Line to Oregon,' Jim continued.

Ted shook his head.

'It's my belief,' he said, 'that the stallion's come from Oregon, and would again visit these parts if he was just driven over the border country.'

Ted's voice faltered as once again he stared across the desert at Wild Horse Bench.

'Then there ain't much we can do,' Jim said in dismay.

There was a short pause.

'Mebbe there is one way it can be done. . . . '

Ted spoke thoughtfully, squatting back on his heels, aware that Jake was now awake and listening to all that was being said.

'What way?' Jim tried to keep his voice level.

'We might try drivin' the stallion so far across the State Line that it 'ud be too far fer him to return again. . . . There's good hunting for the likes o' himself in Oregon.'

'But it would take weeks to get him so far inside Oregon,' Jim protested.

'You want to save the hoss?'

'Why yes. . . . That's all I have in mind right now.'

'Then what does time matter? It wasn't made for young men like yourself . . . nor yet fer lithesome stallions. . . .'

Ted spoke, with a smile on his wrinkled face and a twinkle in his eyes.

'Now gettin' back to the Ghost Hoss! It mightn't take so long after all. . . . That one has bin into Oregon before. . . . He ain't no stranger to the ole wagon trail west either. It's like this, Jim, lad. If we could drive him into the Big Butte country, ye'd see no more of him in these parts. . . .'

'How do you know all this?'

Colorado Ted smiled again confidently.

'I've bin most places,' he replied.

'That he has,' said Jake suddenly, rolling himself out of his blankets. 'But, we'll eat first and talk second.'

*   *   *   *   *

After breakfast, all three sat cross-legged around the fire trying to think out a plan that would not only save the Pahute stallion from death, but also put him well outside the persecution of other ranchers and stockmen.

'I'm willin' to hit the desert trail to Wild Hoss Bench with you both,' Ted said finally. 'There's a back trail up to Oregon. I only found it for myself a month or two back. We could drive the hoss an' his band that way.'

Jim Blaine was doing some quick thinking. He turned to Jake: 'Can you back trek to Rebel Creek for them supplies my father said he'd have sent up? You can then sort of hint you're hittin' the trail west . . . not saying exactly where, an' we can meet some place over the State Line. Ted an' I can somehow manage to get them hosses on the move. I'm sure of it. What you do say, Jake?'

There was a pleading note in Jim's voice as he spoke, which the cowman could not resist. Although he would have preferred to have travelled on to Wild Horse Bench, he agreed to return to Rebel Creek.

Thus was arranged the plan that all three men hoped would protect the notorious Ghost Horse and save him from a fate as bad as that which had overtaken his sire.

In less than an hour, the camp-fire was stamped out. Jake set off on the back trek to Rebel Creek, while Jim Blaine and Colorado Ted—the greatest protector of wild life in the Middle

West—took the desert trail to Wild Horse Bench.

Once again, a new phase in Wild Horse History was in the making.

*   *   *   *   *

Once in the canyons of the mysterious mountain outcrop, Ted was not long in discovering a suitable camping site, and after watering and tethering their horses, Jim and he succeeded between them in lighting a small fire. They then prepared for an exceedingly chilly stay in the solitudes of Wild Horse Bench.

Night came down rapidly. Where the first of the spiral trails thrust upwards, there was soon a deep gloom. Jim, peering up at the last of the light visible in the sky, saw what appeared to be no more than a zig-zag crack in the rock face, and above the serrated ridge itself, that curious caprock above which the first stars were shining brightly.

He was never quite sure afterwards exactly what happened. It seemed that by some miracle, his vision had become extended, and he could see more clearly than anything else that platform of rock surmounting Wild Horse Bench. There was, moreover, a slight lingering of daylight beyond it so that the edge of the rock was drawn in stark lines against the sky.

His breath came shuddering through his half-open lips. It seemed that something was standing on that caprock—just as it had stood once before, long ago.

He lifted his arm, pointing upwards.

Colorado Ted's eyes searched along the wall of the mountain, finally centreing on the platform still sharply visible against the dying light of the sky and the first stars.

One name only he uttered: 'The Ghost Hoss!'

The very next moment, there was nothing more to be seen.

*   *   *   *   *

Very early next morning, Ted and Jim set out on the spiral trail leading to the caprock. Neither knew quite what to expect. Nor did they know where they might expect to find the Pahute stallion and his band.

Jim, in particular, was nervous and tense. He tried hard to fix in his memory every twist of the ever narrowing trail. Whilst it was past sun-up, the sunlight did not seem to reach that part of the trail he and old Ted were following, and it was not until they came out on to the caprock that they beheld the Black Rock Desert ablaze with sunshine, with the Quinn River afar off glistening and shimmering like silver amidst the yellow.

Ted suddenly dismounted and stood on the very edge of the rock staring down the western slopes of Wild Horse Bench.

He grinned as if with great satisfaction, then called Jim over to his side.

'That ole hoss,' said he, 'ain't no fool. T'was him last night up here, an' he smelt the smoke from our camp-fire. See Jimmie, my bright boy, he's already hit the back trail into the mountains . . . drivin' his band in orderly fashion too. . . .'

He shook his head, 'He's a wise one all right. He ain't to be driven out by no man. No sir! Not that one! He's going on 'is own, an' if my guess is right, he'll go right up into them hills an' take the tunnel trail through the eastern spurs to Oregon.'

'Is it goin' to make it easy for us?' Jimmie asked anxiously.

'It sure is, sonny,' Ted answered. 'We'll follow him, an' keep him on the move. Mebbe, after all, we'll get him over the State Line an' keep him goin' westward.'

Jim's eyes, now accustomed to every change on the floor of the canyon below, watched the slow movement of horses up into the hills. Treading behind the band with caution and dignity, was the Ghost Hoss. It could be no other. Even from the caprock on Wild Horse Bench, there could be no mistaking him. There he was—with his white tail and mane . . . the very stallion his father had sought to tame and who, after having escaped, had yet returned to the ranch to steal once again the mares he coveted.

'He's sure some hoss!' There was reverent awe in Jim's voice. Colorado Ted smiled that queer smile of his.

'He's the greatest now that Blue Streak is dead. . . .'

Jim had no words adequate enough to express what he felt in that moment. All he could do was watch that distant line of wild horses moving up into the fastnesses of the Pine Forest Mountains, and behind them, the one great stallion he sought to preserve for ever. . . .

In his ears was the wild singing of the breeze from off the mountains of the west, while in the east, the sun rose higher and higher into a sky incredibly blue, with the yellow desert stretching as far as the eye could see . . . even far beyond the silver thread of the Quinn River.

He looked at Colorado Ted, then turned his gaze once again to the canyon below and the distant movement of horses.

Never before in all his life had he experienced such a thrill of pure happiness.

It was as though that caprock on Wild Horse Bench was the very summit of the world!

CHAPTER TWENTY-FOUR

THE Pahute stallion had leapt over a boulder and was running. There had been a short pause in the movement of the mares, and he was angered at the delay. Now, he galloped alongside the column of mares and yearlings, nipping the flanks of those who, in their fear, had swung a little out of line and impeded his progress. Before he reached the head of the column, the entire herd was again on the trot, travelling deeper and deeper up the volcanic valley, and pushing steadily in the direction of the scant grazing and the pools that lay so far in the northern tip of the range.

Without seeming to do so, the stallion slackened his pace, letting the band pass on until at last, he was once more in the rear of the column and thus better able to ward off danger from those he sensed were likely to attempt a pursuit.

The stallion had been aware of the penetration of Wild Horse Bench by Jim Blaine and Colorado Ted the moment the camp-fire was lit. His keen nose had caught the scent of wood smoke in the evening air. When he eventually climbed up on to the caprock, testing the atmosphere, his sense of smell guided him unerringly to face the very canyon in which the men had set up camp.

He was not unduly alarmed. This was his own particular line of country. His mares and young stock were safe in a canyon that opened out on to the vast volcanic valley between the eastern and western spurs of the Pine Forest range. Since he was more than merely familiar with the route he must surely take to avoid direct contact with the two men, he had returned quietly to the herd, getting it on the move just as the first light of a new day broke in the east.

Despite the fact that the band had now been on the trot

the best part of four hours, it was still gloomy in the valley. Day here, in this deep defile, was never as bright as elsewhere, for the mountains of the eastern spur overshadowed the glen, and by late afternoon, the main escarpment broke up the western light.

All through the long hours till sunset, the Pahute stallion kept the column of mares moving, and only permitted a short respite when it was dark. In less than an hour, the mares and young stock were once more pushing on up the valley, heading for the volcanic pools and the narrow trail through the mountains to the border territories.

There was a moon that night—a pale shadow of a thing that was little more than a sickle of silver that lay over the summit of Wild Horse Bench.

Even so, it gave sufficient light for the stallion to keep his mares under close surveillance. More than that, he was able to pause occasionally and gaze back along the track. Not that he actually feared his would-be pursuers, but he regretted having to leave Wild Horse Bench which of late he had come to regard as his own special hide-out.

He had felt very safe there, but sensed now, that never again could the mountain offer him the security he desired for himself and his band. Men had discovered his ranging territory, and since he was all too keenly aware that he had offended the laws of man, there was only one thing he could do, and that was put as great a distance between himself and the ranchers as was possible.

His move north therefore, while entirely for his own preservation, was as much in keeping with Colorado Ted's plans as anything could be. Moreover, the farther the stallion pressed on up the volcanic valley, the more did he become aware that he was leaving Nevada for ever. This conviction grew stronger in him as his varied memory patterns began to bring into shape the old trail north of the State Line. Soon he was remembering every detail of it, remembering too the pass through the Steens Mountains, and beyond the pass, that wide desert horizon and another mountain outcrop like Wild Horse Bench. . . .

Gradually, he began to shape his entire strategy with a view to making for this distant refuge. He felt that he might even lose his pursuers in this back-mountain hinterland, and once through the narrow trail crossing the eastern hills and over the State Line, he could move his band at will towards the new grazing he felt existed in the Big Butte country.

*   *   *   *   *

Another day came and went, with the stallion more often than not moving alongside the column of mares and yearlings in a long-striding gallop. Then at long last the volcanic pools and the strip of rough grazing came into sight, and since Pahute could not pick up the scent of his pursuers, he let the mares and young stock bed down and rest.

The worst part of the journey was yet to come!

Meanwhile, at Colorado Ted's expressed determination not to stampede the stallion, the two men kept very much in the rear of the wild horse herd. The trail was easy enough to follow without getting too close to the column. More important, the weather remained consistent. The only difficulty was that water supplies were running short, but as Ted remarked, it would not be long before they could have water a-plenty when they reached the area of the volcanic pools.

They could rest awhile too in the spot, for there was grazing for their horses. . . .'that is,' Ted explained, 'if the stallion is not laying up there for a rest. . . .'

However, by the time Ted and Jim reached the waterholes, the Pahute stallion had passed on up the trail to the tunnel-like track that struck through the mountains towards Trident Peak on the border country.

Ted was highly satisfied. He knew now, without the shadow

of a doubt, that the stallion had taken the newly formed trail that he, himself, had so recently discovered. It was also just possible that once over the mountains, the stallion would strike due north, and driving his band across the State Line, take the old wagon trail west.

In the meantime, Pahute was making good progress along the gloomy corridor through the eastern mountain spur. The band, not being pressed too hard, moved quietly and without any display of nervousness. Some of the older mares who had come along the corridor before were, more by luck than judgement, in the lead.

As before, there was a keen wind funnelling up the cleft carrying varying scents. Pahute's nostrils tested it constantly, and always did it tell him the same story—that of long stretches of rangeland and mountain country.

He knew now that he was making a very wise move. There was greater freedom for him and his kind in that vast country across the State Line. Not that he knew it as border country. He only knew it as a mountainous area lying beyond the great white peak that was Trident.

In addition, he was remembering with great clarity of the times he had travelled the deserted wagon trail. Never a sign of man had he ever seen on it . . . only the lost mares he had rounded up.

Pahute tossed his head approvingly. He was filled with a new confidence. He almost scorned being pursued by those he had discovered camping in one of the canyons of Wild Horse Bench. This country he was bent on reaching was not man country. It was made for him and those others who lived by one law—the survival of the fittest!

He paused for a few minutes while the mares and young stock continued to press on along the corridor. The walls of the mountains reared high above him. There was nothing here for him to fear.

Once again did he test the wind currents blowing down the

cleft from the north, and once more was he excited by what he learnt. The last few months were being erased by the older memory patterns . . . all bringing to life the lush grassland about Trout Creek River, and that lonely, western trail, striking through the pass in the Steens Mountains.

He was suddenly very anxious to reach it, and press on to that more distant country where a lone pile of castellated rock rose from out of the yellow and red desert.

Pahute trumpeted his excitement. The column of mares heard it, and those in the lead, quickened their paces.

By nightfall, the band had reached the end of the corridor, and bedded down for the night on the plateau set a full five thousand feet above the valley that widened out to the border territories on the Nevada—Oregon boundary.

* * * * *

Neither Colorado Ted nor Blaine were quite sure of the time they had actually been on the trail before they finally met up with Jake.

The cowman had been successful in obtaining the necessary supplies, and had also managed to hit the trail north into Oregon the day after Ted and Jim had passed along it. What was also of some importance, Jeff Blaine had sent up to Rebel Creek two pack horses, and thus they were now well equipped for the long trek into western Oregon.

There was not the slightest difficulty in determining the trail Pahute was taking. Hoof marks and droppings were everywhere in evidence, and Ted remarked that the stallion was clearly gifted with good sense in that he was following the course of the Trout Creek River towards the pass through the Steens and Pueblo Mountains.

'He's keepin' to well-stocked waterholes an' river grazin' as much as he possibly can,' the old-timer remarked one morning, after a careful examination of the ground.

Jake, every bit as wise as Colorado Ted in reading the signs, was in agreement.

'It looks to me as if you might be right,' the cowman said drily.

Ted looked at him a trifle suspiciously.

'Oh, don't be takin' me up wrong,' Jake added quickly. 'What I mean is just that the stallion, while keepin' them mares on the move, is also keepin' them well fed for that trail through the mountains. There ain't much for them there till they hits the canyon country.'

'Ever bin through the pass yerself?' Ted inquired.

'Nope, but I've heard tell of it from some old-timer who was a wagon master years ago.'

Jim Blaine, till then only concerned with keeping the stallion on the move, asked if it weren't just possible that Pahute might hide up in one of the canyons Jake had mentioned.

'He sure might at that,' Ted answered promptly, 'but we've to see to it that he don't. The Big Butte country is his future home. No other place will do. Stockmen in Nevada might be safe from him then. . . .'

'Any chance of gettin' my Dad's mares?' Jim asked.

Both men shook their heads emphatically.

And Jim never mentioned the mares again, understanding it was wiser not to.

The next few days were the hardest any man had spent on any trail. While Ted and Jake scarcely uttered a word of complaint, Jim found it almost unbearable to remain for such long hours at a stretch in the saddle.

Quite unknown to the three men, Pahute had managed to discover that they were following up in the rear. He made the discovery soon after he had driven the mares and yearlings into one of the canyons abounding Trout Creek River.

It was early evening, and Pahute had taken a stand on one of the higher outcrops, staring back along the trail towards the curve of the river. As at Wild Horse Bench, he got the scent of wood smoke strong in his nostrils. When at last the afterglow of the sunset streamed out across the foothills in the direction of Blue Mountain, he discerned, away off, the movement of horses, quiet at their grazing. He then saw the smoke from the camp-fire.

He remained on the outcrop until it was dusk, then returned to the band. Pahute was not greatly alarmed. Because the men were still some distance away, and not pressing on as others had done in the past, he sensed, dimly, that they were not altogether intent on dispersing the herd and capturing him.

Even so, having long since got the full measure of man and his many nefarious activities, he was taking no chances. He got the herd moving very early next morning. Before sun-up, the entire band was leaving the area of Trout Creek River and turning in towards the deep frown of the pass between the Pueblo and the Steens Mountains.

From then on, Pahute's one concern was to drive the mares and young stock as hard as he possibly could. He was relentless in his purpose, sensing that only very short resting periods could be allowed until the final lay-up in the canyon he himself had once frequented for water. After that, the band would have to face the track across the desert to the far-off mountain that lay out in the west . . . the mountain that was the first of the Big Buttes.

The old wagon trail had not changed since last he trod it. There was still not a vestige of grass or scrub, and there, as if pointing the way through the divide were the remains of the old discarded wagon, while nearby, the half-circle of the wheel still cast a crooked shadow upon the ground.

He had grown very wise indeed—this Pahute. He remembered the caution with which he had approached the divide and entered between the stark, uprising cliffs.

After making a careful survey of the distance that lay between himself and the winding river course, and seeing no sign of man or animal on the almost straight trail that led the way back, he went to the head of the herd.

By late afternoon, he had passed the bleached skull of the elk, with the antlers like the whitened branches of a dead tree, and once more experienced a queer sense of fear at the huddled shape of the grizzly, little more than fur and bone, crouched like a man from out of the past over a boulder equally as ancient.

From that point on, the stallion forced the pace. The band, pressing close at his heels, seemed as anxious as he to reach the shelving walls of the cliffs that marked the western extremity of the pass.

At last was the place, safe in the mountains, where the stallion intended the band should lay up for the night, and possibly for the next day also if there were no signs of pursuit.

He accordingly turned away from the old trail and pressed on up into the canyon that struck far into the northern fastnesses of the mountains.

That night, under the bright western stars, and the moon now a full shield of gold in the sky, the mares and young stock rested under the cotton trees, having grazed well on grass the like of which they had not encountered since leaving Trout Creek River.

Pahute himself, however, was in no mood for rest, despite the effort he had made to reach this most delectable spot. The stallion was standing guard on the wide plateau that dominated the northern slopes of the mountains. He remained silent and motionless throughout the night, until the moon went down and the stars faded. Then he saw the new day come up in the east, with wide spreading fingers of light reaching out across the hills until they finally touched with gold the castellated rock way out in the desert of the west.

The stallion's long journey was nearing its end!

CONCLUSION

IT WAS a perfect morning—that morning when Pahute stood on the northern plateau that dominated the entire out-thrust of the Steens Mountains. As the light gathered and spread, and the last star died, the numerous small ravines and deeply recessed canyons were clearly revealed. Because he had chosen his vantage point so well, he could see into the particular glen in which his herd was now grazing, and at the mouth of the sloping valley, a glimpse of the Oregon Trail beyond which rose the fluted red cliffs of the Pueblo Mountains.

Pahute was well content with all he saw that morning. Part of his contentment came from the fact that he was fully aware that shortly now, he would be on another plateau—the caprock of the immense butte he was intent on reaching and where he and his herd could remain in safety for all time.

He turned his head and looked over his shoulder into that western land of desert and scrub. It seemed that the early morning sunlight, so limpid and clear, had marked out with greater emphasis the unwavering line of the ancient trail.

The stallion could trace its course with the utmost ease. Viewed from so high a position as the plateau, it appeared as a firmly set track stretching out into the yellow and red desert and leading, without deviation, to that far off mountain butte that was so reminiscent of Wild Horse Bench way back in Nevada.

Because the morning light was minute by minute becoming so much stronger, Pahute could discern the outcrop quite distinctly. His nostrils opened wide. As his inward excitement grew, his ears twitched and his white tail rose a little.

The butte had the appearance of increasing in stature, but each dark terrace continued to possess no definite line of demarcation or symmetry. The whole outcrop merely stood out against the blue of the sky, forming into a substantial and fluted mountain that filled Pahute with a restless desire to be on his way.

Then an eddying wind from out of the east passed over him. In the very moment that it touched him, ruffling his mane and tail, he moved his gaze from contemplation of the distant mountain and stared direct into the sunrise.

As his eyes became accustomed to the golden glare, still no sight of man or animal could he see, but there was a stain in the wind that disturbed him . . . a strong stain. . . .

Suddenly he sprang into action. He was suspicious, suspicious of something he could not see, but which the wind told him existed. Treading with caution, he descended from the plateau. In less than thirty minutes, he was back with the mares and yearlings, and was marshalling them into some resemblance of order.

It was then that Colorado Ted and Jake, followed by Jim and the two pack horses, hove into view at the mouth of the canyon.

Despite the strong scent in the wind that had roused his suspicions, the stallion was none the less very surprised at the sudden appearance of those he thought he had shaken off.

The men themselves were even more startled. They had somehow assumed that with the sunrise, Pahute and his band were proceeding to the mountain out in the desert. Their intention had been to travel on to the edge of the divide to ensure that the stallion and his mares were indeed well set on that west-bound trail.

What followed was an instinctive reaction on the part of Pahute. Indeed, he no more than responded to the sudden surge in his blood that, once before, had enabled him to confound a pack of hungry wolves bent on destroying some of his wayward yearlings.

Colorado Ted possessed a somewhat different memory of

what, after all, had been a very similar event. It was connected with Blue Streak who, to protect his herd, had driven it back on those who sought to make him and his mares captive.

Because he possessed so vivid a vision of that scene which had been related to him by one of the ranchers concerned in the episode, his reactions were as quick and instinctive as Pahute's.

He swung his horse about, literally forcing Jim and Jake to take refuge behind a shoulder of rock.

The next few minutes were such that not one of the three men was quite able to ascertain what had actually saved them from death.

By some means or other, quite unknown to the men, the stallion had succeeded in getting the entire band racing swiftly down the canyon. Pahute himself was well in the lead when the racing mares and yearlings surged out into the pass.

Here, the stallion, regardless of any injury he might sustain, swung in close to the out-jutting shoulder of rock behind which the three were hiding. The men's horses were badly frightened at the close approach of the wild stallion, but due to Jim's expert handling of them, did not attempt a break-away.

Just when it seemed that Pahute must dash himself against the ragged cliff, he galloped out into the pass. Trumpeting loudly, he had the herd racing wild-eyed down the trail in the direction of the western limits of the divide. The uprising fangs of the mountains that guarded the trail from east to west, ranged away on either side, each cliff red and deeply scarred like some Indian ornamentation that had no place in reality but only in mythology.

By now, the stallion was following up in the rear. Still screaming loudly, and plunging dangerously when one or other of the mares almost stumbled with terror, he drove the band to an even greater pace.

He had no pity for any who might show weakness in this moment of danger. His one aim was to get the band out into the desert and on to the trail where movement would be less restricted than in the confined space of the pass.

In less than ten minutes from the time when the wild horse band burst out from the canyon, Pahute had achieved his purpose. The mares were streaming out into the desert in a tossing line, the foremost animals striking out across the old Oregon Trail that led into the yellow void and the far off mountain that was Beaty's Butte.

Seldom before had such a stampede taken place, and certainly never had one been attempted by a stallion who had but one purpose—to outrun those who had dared to come up on him so stealthily.

Blaine and his companions had been very much shaken by the stallion's unexpected manoeuvre. Indeed, they had not realized that he had been hiding up in the canyon. They had entered the last part of the divide under cover of darkness, proceeding with caution so as not betray their presence to the horse whom they had felt was, at sunrise, striking out into the desert to Beaty's Butte.

It was fully an hour after the stampede that they decided to ride on to the western limits of the pass.

They rode the last of the old trail through the mountains in silence. Each man was busy with his thoughts. At last they reined in their mounts under the enormous cliffs that guarded the western extremity of the divide. Before them was the ribbon-like unfurling of the ancient Oregon Trail, striking out across the desert Badlands.

Far over, rising like the purple of smoke against the lighter blue of the morning sky, was the immense butte. By shading their eyes and limiting the range of their vision, the three travellers could see it more clearly as a castellated rock, surely a fitting refuge for any wild horse herd, and certainly an impregnable stronghold for a stallion the like of Pahute—the Ghost Hoss.

As they withdrew their gaze from the butte and concentrated

on the desert itself, they could see, far out, a finger of rock dividing the trail, and whirling up about the curious obelisk, a pall of dust.

'There they go,' said Colorado Ted softly.

'Headin' right for the butte,' Jake answered with satisfaction.

Jim Blaine could not speak. Their plan had come off—beyond even their wildest expectations. He had the distinct feeling that never again would the Ghost Hoss range the Nevada territories.

With a vague regret in his heart, he watched the rising cloud of dust, saw it drift farther and farther away until it was no more than a haze on the skyline that finally obscured the outline of Beaty's Butte.

Then he said tonelessly: 'Come! Let's be headin' back along the trail.'

The others turned their horses about in silence. All three considered they had surely seen the last of Pahute—the son of Blue Streak. Both Jake and Ted, like Jim, felt that never again would the stallion return to raid the ranchlands of Nevada.

As they started to ride back through the pass, Jim half-raised himself in the saddle and looked back once more.

It seemed that nerveless fingers were clutching at his heart, increasing the regret he felt at the end of what had surely been a magnificent adventure.

He had no remembrance of his father's mares just then. He thought only of the stallion.

The haze of dust continued to rise on the horizon, clearly indicative that the herd of wild horses, driven by the Ghost Horse was still on the move. . . .

EPILOGUE

EVERY bit of twenty-five years ago—that quitting of Nevada by the Ghost Hoss and his band. Jim Blaine, that much older too, conscious of his rapidly beating heart and the highly nervous appearance of his two horses, stood close against the finger of rock staring out across the desert and Beaty's Butte.

The half-light had changed little in the few minutes that had bridged the present and the past. The banners of colour still flamed over the mountains of the west, and the stars remained pale like the twinkling lamps of some slow-moving wagon train in the sky.

This could not be happening, of course. It was all a dream, brought about by the long time he had spent in the saddle and the thoughts he had been conjuring up of the past when he and Jake, in the company of old Colorado Ted, had pursued the Pahute stallion and his herd to the pass way back in the Steens Mountains.

Only once before had he come this far into the desert, and that was all of twenty years ago, just before he had married a neighbouring rancher's daughter and settled down. Nothing had happened then. In a moment, he would surely come out of his dreaming!

Just then, Blinker whinnied with terror and pressed in closer to his master. Boxer, the pack horse, did the same. Both animals were sweating with fear.

Blaine suddenly caught both animals by their manes, and dragged them, plunging, to the security of the finger-like obelisk. He continued to hang on to them, with anxiety in his grip. His long knowledge of horses told him more surely than anything else that something unusual was indeed happening . . . that a herd of wild horses was approaching. . . .

His one clear impression as he hung on to the horses was a further glimpse of the new moon lying over the serrated peaks of the Pueblo Mountains.

Then he heard the pounding of hooves.

The sound came nearer and nearer, the rising dust over the desert becoming more like an enormous cloud. Then out of the thickening haze appeared a band of racing mares and making unerringly due east in the direction of the pass.

Running first to one side of the band, then to the other, was a great stallion with a silver mane and tail that made his steel-blue flanks and back seem strangely out of keeping with the rest of him. He was no mere mustang—this stallion with such distinctive markings. He possessed all the signs of good breeding, surely the very same breeding that, in the past, had made the names of Blue Streak and Diablo names of the purest magic in the ears of the old-timers who had roamed the Oregon Trail.

The stallion was screaming, driving his mares faster and faster towards the far off shadows of the eastern mountains where night was slowly setting up its tents.

With increasing rapidity, the band and the stallion approached the uprising rock behind which Jim Blaine and his two horses were sheltering.

Then, almost as if by long experience gained over many years, the herd separated, streaming past the rocky obstacle in two columns that, in the very tenseness of the moment, defied all description. There were reds, blacks, bays and dappled mares in the serried throng, all racing as fleet as the wind.

The dust continued to rise, almost obscuring the band. Just when it seemed that nothing more could possibly be seen because of the density of the cloud, the stallion himself appeared, coming up out of the queer half-light like some winged figure of mythology, rearing and plunging with mingled delight and savagery.

He broke abruptly the pace he had been making, halting

practically alongside the obelisk. Swinging about, he faced the west—a magnificent silhouette of everything a great horse should be.

He gazed back at the distant butte now ringed with the last glow of the sunset.

Suddenly he reared, beating the air, his forelegs rising and falling as if he were bent on pulling down the very stars and trampling them under foot. Once again he sent his eerie bugle-call echoing across the silent corridors of the Big Butte country.

An instant more, and he had turned. Screaming defiance to any who would oppose him, he set off after the mares. As he got into a long, swinging stride, he became a racing shape of exceptional power and beauty . . . so clearly a descendant of that other legendary stallion, Diablo, who was said to have possessed a human tongue and spoke to his Apache master in a language he understood.

Any Apache seeing him then, or indeed any of the old-timers who occasionally visited the west, would have declared at once as Jim Blaine was prepared to swear later, that the stallion was none other than Pahute—the Ghost Hoss of the Oregon Trail. . . .

At the second of his galloping past, Blaine was conscious more of awe than actual fear. Still retaining a firm grip on the manes of his two horses, he tried in vain to marshal his thoughts into some recognizable pattern. He endeavoured to turn his head to stare back along the trail. This too he was unable to do.

Swiftly then, the sound of pounding hooves died away. Suddenly, quite suddenly so it seemed, they could no longer be heard. There was a curious silence . . . no sound whatever reaching up from out of the gloom. Not even the faintest ripple of wind disturbed the desert. Moreover, the suspended half-light was withdrawn, and it was dark, with no afterglow anywhere. . . .

More Beaver Books

We hope you have enjoyed this Beaver Book. Here are some of the other titles:

A Knight and his Castle What it was like to live in a castle, by R. Ewart Oakeshott

The Twelve Labours of Hercules The adventures of the hero Hercules, beautifully retold by Robert Newman; illustrated superbly by Charles Keeping

Travel Quiz A brain-teasing quiz book for all the family on all aspects of travel by plane, train and car

My Favourite Animal Stories Sad, funny and exciting stories about all sorts of animals, chosen and introduced by Gerald Durrell

Who Knows? Twelve unsolved mysteries involving sudden death, mysterious disappearances and hidden treasure, by Jacynth Hope-Simpson

The Call of the Wild The epic story of Buck the great sledge dog in the frozen North, by Jack London

The Last of the Vikings Henry Treece's exciting story, in the saga tradition, about the young Harald Hardrada, King of Norway; with more superb illustrations by Charles Keeping

New Beavers are published every month and if you would like the *Beaver Bulletin* – which gives all the details – please send a stamped addressed envelope to:

Beaver Bulletin
The Hamlyn Group
Astronaut House
Feltham
Middlesex TW14 9AR

340074